MARTIAN GIRL

JACKIE HUNTER

I dedicate this book with love to
Raymond Lambert.

ACKNOWLEDGMENTS

I would like to acknowledge my Alpha and Beta Readers, Jessica and Debbie for their positive and critical feedback. Also special thanks to my cousin, Phyllis Rippy Green, and my forever friend and mentor: Greg Smith, author of *Agile Writer Method* and founder of Agile Writers of Richmond, Virginia for their critiques.

You have helped me to create a story that all ages will enjoy reading.

CONTENTS

Chapter 1 – I Don't Want to Go to Earth 1

Chapter 2 – The Visitors from Earth 11

Chapter 3 – Martian Caves are Not Safe............................ 43

Chapter 4 – Is This Where We Sleep? 61

Chapter 5 – Extraterrestrials 79

Chapter 6 – Arguments 99

Chapter 7 – Where Is the Et?............................ 109

Chapter 8 – What a Party! 117

Chapter 9 – More Than a Karate Lesson 131

Chapter 10 – You're Not My Friend 139

Chapter 11 – Nightmares 153

Chapter 12 – So, This Is a Meat Lab 167

Chapter 13 – Drowning In My Space Suit............................ 177

Chapter 14 – Europa 195

Chapter 15 – The Asteroid 211

Chapter 16 – We Don't Belong Here 227

Chapter 17 – Celine's Plan 241

Chapter 18 – Taken 251

Chapter 19 – Trapped 259

Chapter 20 – Earth and Mars Space Forces............................ 267

Chapter 21 – The Interrogation............................ 277

Chapter 22 – Martians On Earth............................ 291

Chapter 23 – The Artemis Experience 297

CHAPTER 1

I DON'T WANT TO GO TO EARTH

On Earth, the Red Cloud family had been summoned to the home of Catori Red Cloud. She was a woman of great wisdom, a mystic, an elder, and the Beloved Woman of her family. Her doctors had given her six months to live, so she had called her clan together to give them the sad news. However, last night, she had a dream about her granddaughter, Celine, her youngest grandchild, and the only one she had not met in person because Celine lived on Mars.

In her dream, she saw her granddaughter staring into the face of a hideous creature. It was like none that Catori had ever seen before. She could feel her granddaughter's fear. She believed she had the dream because the ancestors wanted her to share it with the clan so that they would use their collective powers to protect her.

Hundreds of family members stood in the large clearing, nearly forty acres of land. Her son, Wohali, helped her to the platform that had been temporarily built in front of her home, a 3-D printed fabricated log cabin. She was tall and muscular despite her age. Her proud, calm face was untouched by stem treatments. Everyone became silent as the Beloved Woman looked with admiration at her people. Like the gray wolf that came back from extinction, so had they.

"May the warm winds of Heaven blow softly upon our clan. May the Great Spirit bless all who are here," she said. She spoke with authority, loud and clear, her voice needed no technical enhancements.

"Wado," they replied, in unison, which is 'thank you' in the Cherokee language.

"All of you know that I have summoned you here to say my farewells."

Some of the women rubbed their hands together, fighting back tears. The men stood there stone-faced.

"However. The Great Spirit and the ancestors have given me a dream to share with you. Last night I saw my granddaughter, Celine."

A heavy woman sitting in the front row whispered, "Celine, that's Adohi's child. You remember he settled on Mars."

"In this dream, Celine was face to face with a being that was neither human nor animal," Catori said. She paused, waiting for her words to sink in.

One woman raised her hand to her mouth, "Oh how awful."

A second one whispered, "Her dreams cannot be taken lightly."

Then there was silence. Wohali, who had been standing close to his mother's side, spoke up.

"What does this mean? What can we do, mother?"

"Tell my son, Adohi, that I want to meet my granddaughter. Tell him to send her to Earth where she will be safe in the protection of her tribe.

"Yes, we will protect her," men and women shouted.

Wohali gently laid his hand on his mother's shoulder. "I will ask my brother to send her," he said.

On Mars, the voices of the Cherokee people floated above Catori's sleeping grandchild.

Celine's eyes popped open. *What's happening?* She thought she heard hundreds of voices surrounding her. They sounded like the electronic bees in the greenhouse beehive. There was one word she could make out though, adasdelvdi, which means protect in Cherokee. Only her grandma spoke to her in Cherokee. *Why were they saying that?*

"Adasdelvdi! Adasdelvdi!" The word was pounding in her head like a drumbeat.

Protect who? Grandma! Something's wrong with Grandma!

Celine peered over her covers looking at the speaker on the metallic wall next to her small desk. She had not heard from her grandmother in over an Earth's week. *Why hasn't she called me?* The future Media Star had been so busy recording her Martian Girl Media show that she hadn't noticed the absence of her grandma's call. A feeling of dread washed over her. She slipped out of her metal bunk, hopping on the large sofa bunk beneath it and then to the hard cold floor. Shivering, she wrapped her thin arms around her shoulders and moved quickly to her polished desk where her small computer rested.

"Uji," she said to wake her computer and her AI. "Call Grandma Enisi."

The AI hologram appeared instantly. Her pale appearance and brown-colored hair reminded Celine of her mom when her mom lived on Mars.

"On it."

It would take twenty minutes for the Mars to Earth connection, just enough time for her to take her dry shower, and to get a quick breakfast. She took her goggles from one of the drawers beneath the sofa bunk and snapped them around her head.

"Blue light shower," she said as she stood erect in the grey jumpsuit, she had slept in.

Instantly the only light in the windowless room began humming and emitting 470 nm waves of blue light from the ceiling. Celine closed her eyes and tilted her head back. The blue light as it exterminated any germs on her, or her jumpsuit gave her some desperately needed warmth. The Compound was always cold, however, today felt even colder.

After a few minutes, the noisy shower stopped, and Celine removed her goggles. She checked her eyes in the polished metal mirror on the wall above her desk. Her mom had said it distorted her image, but to Celine who had never used a glass mirror, everything was perfect. Her contacts were doing their job, hiding her natural eyes that sometimes glowed like that of a feline in the dark. Dr. Baylor, Celine's doctor, had told Celine that her eyes were a blessing.

"If they're a blessing, why am I wearing contacts to hide them?" she had asked Dr. Baylor who quickly answered, "They're not for you. They're for the colonists. They don't need to know all of your secrets."

Yes, secrets were a way of life in her family. Her father had kept secrets about his eyes, and she didn't know that she had inherited her special eyes from him until she was twelve. Her mom had kept secrets too because she wanted Celine to feel like a normal Earth girl. Nothing about Celine was like a normal Earth girl. She was the first human born on Mars. Never having to deal with the full force of Earth's gravity or the brightness of its sun, she was lanky and bright lights bothered her.

After a quick breakfast of yellow and brown Tofu mush, Celine rushed back through the narrow halls to her quarters to talk with her grandma, however, she was surprised to find her dad and Rachel, her stepmom waiting for her in her tiny quarters. Her dad's eyes were red and watery. Her usually cheerful stepmom sat gazing at her hands as her thumbs massaged her large belly.

"It's grandma, isn't it," said Celine as she caught her breath.

"Yes," said her father. "Your grandma has had heart failure." He whispered. Celine could barely hear him. *How? No one has more heart!*

"I don't understand."

Her father covered his face with both of his hands. *Dad, you're scaring me.*

Rachel spoke up. "Your grandma might be transitioning soon. She wants, we want, your dad and I, want you to meet her before it's too late."

Celine dropped down on the bunk between her parents. They wrapped their arms around her, and they cried.

The next morning, a knock at the door startled Celine awake. She groggily made her way to the entrance to see who was awaiting her. It was Dr. Baylor, with a large black medical bag. A bit confused, Celine rubbed her eyes and snapped out of her sleepy daze, inviting Dr. Baylor into the unit.

"Your father told me about your grandmother. I'm so sorry."

Celine took a long breath. She noticed the doctor's large medical bag.

"Thank you," she mumbled.

"You will need to be strong enough to endure Earth's gravity and atmospheric pressure," the doctor explained as she began unpacking a weighted vest from the medical bag.

The Compound was pressurized, and the community utilized artificial gravity, but the forces were still not as strong as those on Earth. Celine had also spent much time beyond the confines of the Compound on Mars' surface, which had but a third of Earth's gravity and less than one percent of Earth's atmospheric pressure.

Though Dr. Baylor spoke warmly, Celine could hear a graveness in her tone.

You're a strong Martian, her dad had always told her, but she'd have to be a bit stronger to manage on Earth. Celine stared at the 15-kilogram weighted vest, dreading the thought of having to wear it.

Dr. Baylor put the vest across Celine's shoulders and snapped the fasteners and belt around her waist. Celine thought the vest was so appropriate, heavy like her heart.

"You only need to wear it three hours a day."

Wow. Can anything get worse?

Later that afternoon, Celine's dad came by to check on her and to give her devastating news. She would be traveling to Earth without him and Rachel since their baby was due in two months.

"It's just not safe to have a baby in deep space," he explained as the spirit in Celine's eyes fizzled out. "But you'll have Mando with you… Anna and Nina will be there, too."

Celine rolled her eyes and flopped onto the bunk.

"I know the twins can be a bit troublesome," Celine's father continued, "but at least you'll have a few familiar faces to keep you grounded."

"When do I leave?" Celine asked in a lifeless tone.

"Very shortly after the Fantasy lands."

With a straight face, Celine offered her dad a single head nod in response. Despite Celine's nonverbal response, her father figured there'd be some lingering confusion, so he went on to explain that the Fantasy—a luxury spaceship, as the name might imply—was scheduled to arrive in thirty days' time with a handful of visitors from Earth on board. Once that visit was over, however, Celine would be accompanying them on their voyage back. Mr. Red Cloud then kissed his daughter on the forehead before seeing himself out.

Celine always figured she would visit Earth at some point. She thought perhaps she'd go in three years to celebrate her sixteenth birthday with her mom. Her mother had always made it clear that she wanted Celine to leave Mars behind and come live with her instead, but Mars was what Celine knew, what she loved, and where she felt safe. Besides, getting to Earth meant having to travel through deep space, and that always carried risks. Plus, Earth itself could prove to be a very dangerous place for a Martian like her. Although these thoughts had always swirled around in Celine's head, they were much more overwhelming now. Her departure date was just one month away, and the circumstances under which she was going on this trip were nowhere near ideal.

Celine peered into the metallic mirror on her wall, the one her mother hated. She studied herself in the mirror, paying close attention to her eyes and the effect the contact lenses had on them. Overall, she definitely looked like an Earthling, albeit a lanky one. However, as she took a few steps away from the mirror, she pinched out the contacts, revealing glowing yellow eyes. Her blessing as Dr. Baylor had called them.

"Humans generally can't even see one percent of the light spectrum," Dr. Baylor had marveled. "But you're special."

Celine put the lenses into a blue-light storage container and then tried to maneuver her way out of the heavily weighted vest. As she wriggled out of the garment, she caught a glimpse of herself and her glowing eyes in the mirror. She sighed. Celine may not have been particularly excited about the trip, but she did hope that once she arrived, she'd be able to fit in with the girls her age down on Earth.

With the vest plopped off onto the floor and her contact lenses safely stored away, Celine opened up the drawer beneath her bunk and took out her flute. It had been intricately carved out of wood and passed down in her father's family for generations. Now the flute was hers, and she often found herself playing it when she felt down or lonely and today was one of those days. If another bad thing happened today, she might go to sleep and never wake up.

She held the flute delicately between her fingers and started to blow a high vibrational tune. Instantly, Ugi—Celine's holographic, AI-based teacher and helper—appeared in front of her. For some reason, Ugi was always summoned when Celine played her flute as if the music somehow connected with her AI on an emotional level.

Celine stared at the aura-less hologram but continued to play, waiting for Ugi to bestow some unwarranted facts about deep space travel, space pirates, or death upon her. Ugi *said* nothing. In fact, the AI appeared to be experiencing pleasure in listening to Celine play. Its eyes appeared closed as if soaking in the melody. Celine closed her eyes, too, and carried on playing the sweet, calming music as tears streamed down her cheeks.

Earth… Ready or not, here I come.

CHAPTER 2

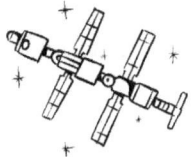

THE VISITORS FROM EARTH

B ehind the camera stood Mando Karr — a Newcomer, the name given to those who recently arrived on Mars. Mando had taken a range of cinematography and film production courses at his high school back on Earth and had agreed to help film for Celine's new media show called Martian Girl.

"Celine, are you sure you feel up to doing this?" he asked.

"I promised Alex, I would do them. He's expecting them to be done here on Mars, not deep space. I've got to get the episodes finished before I leave for Earth."

"Well, if you insist. There's too much shadow on your face. Turn your face toward the light," he instructed.

Celine thought Mando was a good director, however, not as good as Alex. Alex was a popular media Star on Earth. If the recordings needed doctoring, he would know what to do. Trying to take her mind off of her dying grandmother, she turned her melancholy face toward the only light source in the room: a phosphorescent white light embedded in the ceiling.

"Like this," she said and forced a smile.

"Perfect," Mando said as he nodded in approval. "Three. Two. One. Action!"

Celine's long, slender legs tensed up as she pressed her tiny hips against the cold metal stool, trying to find warmth where there was none. She sat tall, counted to five in her head (as Mando had taught her), then flashed a wide fake smile to the camera. She began to speak.

"I love it here," she said in response to a student's pre-submitted question about her home on Mars, which was projected on a hologram screen above the camera. She began reading some of the other questions aloud. "*Do I feel sad because I've never been to Earth?* Well, I can't miss something I've never experienced. Mars is the only planet I've ever lived on. It's my home. So... no."

"Have I ever seen a Martian? I am a Martian," Celine asserted with confidence. She then pondered for a moment. "Well, if being a 'Martian,' you mean a tiny green extraterrestrial, then no... I haven't seen any of those."

She chuckled, but her memories of her experience in the caves of the Chaos region last year quickly came flooding back. Granted, there were no green creatures lurking within the caves, but something or someone had surely lived there long before the colonists had arrived. She remembered the paintings on some of the cave walls that had been destroyed by a mysterious flood. Celine cleared her throat and continued.

"Mars really is the most beautiful planet. Some people think it's like Earth's moon, but it's not. Earth's moon is covered in razor-sharp gray dust and smells like old-fashioned gun- powder. Some of the Newcomers say Mars smells like eggs, but I don't smell anything. Martian soil is as soft as baby powder — it's a lovely shade of orangey-red too!" Her eyes darted around the room, looking for something she could present to the camera that resembled the color of Martian dust, but almost every object in the room was a variation of gray. There was a brief silence until Mando gave Celine a gesture to just keep going.

"Mars also has breathtaking mountains and valleys, just like Earth does. Luckily, though, Mars isn't overpopulated." Celine giggled at her own cheeky comment, as she beamed with Martian pride. "There are only 300 of us here, with the entire planet to ourselves."

However, Celine knew deep down that would soon change. With the recent discovery of the underground lakes and rivers, crowds of Newcomers would be flocking to Mars by the shipload, crowding her beloved planet. Already, two hundred of them have come, and have put a strain on all the life support systems,

Celine hurriedly scanned the screen, trying to decide what to respond to next. "To answer Antonio's question, everyone here on the Compound gets along. People here are very private but still friendly and polite."

Celine swallowed after uttering the words *friendly* and *polite*. These words did once accurately describe the Compound's inhabitants, but that was before the Newcomers arrived.

"Mars to Celine," said Mando. "Everything okay? We can record later."

Mando, despite being a Newcomer (and a bit of a film snob), proved to be a decent, level-headed guy in general. Celine viewed him as the big brother she'd never had. Mando came to Mars with his parents, a pair of botanists who brought thousands of fast-growing Black Leaf saplings to the planet. They were determined to establish a forest around the Compound, and so far, they had done well. He would be returning to Earth when the next spaceship arrived and so would she. At least she'd have a good friend with her while traveling in deep space.

"No, I don't want to record later. I'm expecting a call from Alex, and I want to be finished with this last episode. That way, Alex and I can talk about which parts Earthlings will find interesting, what should be cut out, and the order of the release dates." Celine's eyes twinkled. "After all, Alex is the producer of this whole thing," she told Mando for the hundredth time.

Mando looked down at his grey fabricated fur boots and sucked his teeth. Celine did not notice. The two teens finished the recordings and Celine now had six completed episodes to share with Alex, her co-producer and the best-looking boy on Earth!

Alex was Celine's dear friend, and though she hadn't told him this directly, he held a special place in her heart. Last year he came to Mars with his father. She was initially the only child in the Martian colony, so Alex was the first person around her age she had ever seen in person, let alone befriended. However, Alex accompanied Celine to the treacherous Chaos region and got lost alongside her. Shortly after their miraculous return, Alex left Mars. Celine also noticed that he hadn't produced any new episodes of his adventure series since their ordeal back in the caves, and she felt deeply responsible. *Maybe if he hadn't tried to help me, he'd still be his usual, adventure-loving self.*

Alex and Celine's friendship bond grew stronger before he headed back to Earth, though. They always danced around it, but Celine felt that Mr. Rittenhouse—Alex's overly concerned father and the founder of the Martian colony—likely forbade him from ever returning to the planet, whether or not he wanted to. Nonetheless, the two kept in touch via Alex's weekly calls. It was because of his constant persistence and encouragement that Celine actually decided to proceed with The Martian Girl—a digital series concept Alex came up with and would produce and promote for her from afar.

"You were the first person born on Mars," he had told her. "People want to know about you. You're a mystery, but an interesting one. You're popular, Celine. Earth loves you."

Later that day, Alex called Celine and told her to save the recordings until he returned to Earth. He was going on vacation to Lunar, Earth's moon, to the city of Artemis. Artemis was the place to be during Spring Break: endless parties, otherworldly entertainment, and few rules.

When Celine told him she was coming to Earth, instead of saying he would be happy to see her, he seemed more interested in the date she would be leaving Mars. When she told him she would be leaving on the Fantasy, she thought he caught his breath.

"You will be happy to see me on Earth? She inquired.

"Of course, I will."

Despite his words, Celine felt there was something left unsaid.

"Were you ever planning to return to Mars?"

"Why would you ask that now? I can see you when you come to Earth."

"It's not about me, Alex. It's about you. I was thinking if you could come see how the caves have been modernized, how things have changed, maybe you would do more adventure shows, like before we met. I feel like I've destroyed your career."

Alex went silent for a moment.

"You didn't destroy my career. I have several adventure films in the making.

"Look, Celine. My dad doesn't want me to ever return to Mars."

"When did you start doing what your dad says?

He's already told me that he would disinherit me if I disobeyed him. Sure, I almost died on Mars, but it wasn't your fought. I didn't have to go with you to the Chaos. I had something to proved to my dad. I didn't do a good job of that. So for now, if I were to ever come to Mars, he couldn't know it. He'd disinherit me."

"But if you realized how drastically different the caves, they are now versus how they were back when we got lost, it might be therapeutic."

"My psychologist said that. So now you're a practicing therapist? Hey, I gotta get going. My flight leaves in a few hours, and if I miss it, I won't be able to get another one for at least six days."

"Your flight? You're taking a space shuttle? That's a three-day journey, isn't it?"

"Yes, yes, and yes, it is."

"I would've assumed you'd be taking one of your dad's spaceships. Isn't that a lot faster?"

"We don't own them anymore. Dad sold them to the Space Force—practically gave them away. Gotta go. We'll talk about the cave stuff later."

Yeah, sure we will, Celine scoffed to herself, knowing that Alex constantly avoided talking about their distressing trek through the Chaos region.

Granted, Celine had strong negative feelings about the caves too, but not like Alex. If he could only see all the changes that had been made. The cave floors and walls had been laser-scorched to rid the caves of germs and fungus, so it was said, and a variety of futuristic light fixtures were installed throughout. A water infiltration plant in the region was in the late stages of development, and the construction of safe luxury homes within the caves was currently underway. Some of the homes had pressurized glass-dome-covered patios for roofs, which extended out from the caves and onto the Martian surface and Celine's father had pre-purchased one of the homes. So as soon as the Power Plant was completed, Celine and her family, along with many other colonists, would be moving to this underground city.

Dr. Baylor had talked Celine into returning to the caves to see all the magnificent changes and because of her visit, she was beginning to put all her negative experiences in the caves behind her. She felt safe on Mars. However, she grew up hearing dozens of stories about space pirates and kidnappings near Earth's moon millions of miles away. Now she was going to Earth's moon and then to Earth, far away from the safety of Mars.

The thirty days leading up to the Fantasy's arrival whizzed by so quickly. Dr. Baylor regularly assured Celine that as long as she wore her weighted vest as instructed, she'd be ready for her journey *physically*. However, no one was able to guarantee that Celine would genuinely fit in on Earth. There were only three teens among the Newcomers: Mando and the twins.

The twins — Anna and Nina Emoto — were stunning to look at. They were only 16 years old, yet taller than the general population. They had heart-shaped faces with smooth, supple, cream-colored complexions, and their deep brown, almond-shaped eyes were emphasized by their long, thick lashes. Celine was mesmerized by them. Unlike Celine, who always wore monochromatic gray, Anna and Nina sported different-colored jumpsuits practically every day. It was rare to see the twins without matching wigs and color-coordinated boots. Celine had no idea what Anna and Nina's natural hair color was, but that didn't matter — she had never seen anything so glamorous.

Celine's parents felt that the older teens were poor role models. Still, Celine wanted to be like them. She wanted to be the twins' friend, despite the fact that they compared her skin texture to that of a 'baby armadillo'. Celine had to do a bit of research to find out what this unknown Earth species was, and it took her quite some time to determine the correct spelling. *Armedilo. Armadila. Armudelo.* When Celine finally found a photo of a baby armadillo, she initially thought it was cute. However, she couldn't pinpoint any resemblance this animal had to her, and it ultimately dawned on her that, regardless, the twins likely did not intend for this comparison to be a compliment. That was their nature, though. Anna and Nina were gorgeous and captivating, yet they had a quirky vibe, regularly making offbeat, silly (and vaguely rude) comments that only they could see the humor in.

Celine reflected on the day the girls first arrived at the Martian Compound a few months back. Perfectly in sync, Anna and Nina strutted into the Commons, but there was a lightness about the way that they walked. It was almost as if they were floating. They held their heads high in a regal manner. Their vibrant jumpsuits hugged their slender bodies in a way that greatly flattered their figures, and a sheer, shawl-like wrap flowed from their shoulders. Silence immediately fell over the Commons, as if everyone was awestruck by their beauty. In a sea of gray uniforms were these two beautiful girls, dressed from head to toe in dynamic shades of purple and pink. Celine was elated to learn that Anna and Nina would be sharing her quarters as roommates, but it didn't take long for her excitement to turn into frustration.

The twins revealed their mischievous inclinations early on. A few days after their arrival, Nina, the younger and slightly shorter twin, found her way to the control panel of the Compound's food printer. As the daughter of one of Earth's major tech moguls, Nina was able to virtually cultivate the Carolina Reaper—one of the spiciest chili peppers on Earth—and incorporate it into every single recipe within the pre-programmed daily menu. Nina claimed she wanted to 'add a little spice' to the Martian lifestyle.

Celine had watched as the colonists took their first bites of food and began making distorted faces. She snickered along with the twins as their victims gulped down water and fanned their mouths. However, when Celine saw her pregnant stepmother walk up to the printer to get a meal, it was no longer funny, so she rushed over and stopped her stepmother from eating the tainted food and, in doing so, exposed Nina for what she had done.

The twins remained furious with Celine well after the incident, pinning the blame on her for the week-long grounding they received. Part of the twins' punishment was to spend the majority of their days with their mother so that she could keep a watchful eye on them. She worked as a volcanologist, and her "office" was whatever lava tube—a natural cave formed by flowing lava that has cooled and hardened—she'd been assigned to examine on a given day. After only two days of being forced to tag along with their mother, Anna, and Nina decided that going forward, they would be sleeping in a tent on a soft air mattress within the warm lava tube network. They would *not* be returning to the cold, hard bunk beds in Celine's drab quarters. Celine could not argue that the lava tubes were probably a much warmer place to sleep than her tiny room, but she felt that the underlying reason that the twins did not return was that they did not like her.

Celine remembered when Anna and Nina announced they'd be moving out of her quarters and into the lava tubes.

"We didn't come to Mars to be cooped up for six months in a tiny space dungeon with some outback Martian chick," Nina had said.

She figured the twins were upset but, much like the armadillo comment, it was difficult for Celine to wrap her mind around the negative connotations of some of Anna's words, particularly the term *outback*.

Mars was, in fact, the new outback, and many people referred to it as such: a place with a wealth of uninhabited potential. And, at least in Celine's opinion, that's what made it so special. Being a part of that, furthermore, was a deep-seated source of pride for Celine, so having it used as an insult solidified the idea that she very well might be treated as an outcast upon arriving to Earth, simply for existing.

If it wasn't for Mando, Celine wouldn't have anyone her age to spend time with. Like the twins, he had a six-month Visa to stay on Mars, only essential workers could stay longer. During his six months visit, he taught her the ET Shuffle (a popular dance trend circulating on Earth), and he often shared much of his Indie, nature-advocate-based music collection with her. Sometimes, Mando and his parents would even invite her to help plant the small, young Black Leaf trees. The Karrs, as a familial unit, handled their saplings with love and affection. Celine never thought of treating plants as pets the way the Karrs did, but the plants did seem to thrive in response to the Karrs' attention.

Thanks to the Karrs, the outer area of the Compound was nearly covered with Black Leaf trees sprouting from the red sand, creating a majestic forest effect. Not only were these trees easy on the eyes, but they gave the Compound even more protection from cosmic radiation. The heat emitted from the Compound itself offered warmth for the trees during the freezing cold nights. Celine's dad had called it a "win-win situation," the kind of mutually beneficial dynamic most of the colonists strived for in their developments. Although she appreciated Mando, Celine couldn't shake the desire for this kind of relationship with Anna and Nina. Mando told her that the twins would be traveling on the Fantasy with them when they headed to Earth. Celine thought this might be her chance to become their friend. She could educate them about living a good life on Mars, and in turn, they could teach her about the intricacies of being a teenage girl on Earth.

Today, the Fantasy Spaceship would dock at the small station that orbited the planet, as all incoming ships did; it was much easier to dock in orbit than to try to land on the Martian surface. Aboard the Fantasy were ten extremely wealthy visitors. A decent number of the First Hundred were unenthusiastic about their arrival. They complained that the guests would be unlikely to fulfill any real function for the advancement of Mars and put a strain on the planet's already-strained life support systems. The guests' ten-day visit also came across as voyeuristic in nature to a handful of the Compound residents, and for that, they were not particularly welcome.

Celine had many apprehensions regarding going into deep space for the first time. She had learned about phenomena like cosmic radiation and solar flares, and she feared risks like those could potentially outweigh the reward of visiting Earth. She heard through the grapevine that the Fantasy's walls were filled with water that could absorb normal levels of cosmic radiation, and the ship had special chambers for its passengers during extreme radioactive encounters, including solar flares. This eased her nerves a bit. However, people occasionally hallucinated in deep space due to radiation sensitivity, and Celine worried that her Tetrachromacy (the eye condition that gave her the ability to see things others couldn't) could somehow play into that possibility. As she and other colonists made their way to the Commons to watch the Fantasy dock, she found herself absorbed in fear and worry.

Many of the colonists were already in the Commons by the time Celine arrived. The ship was still orbiting the planet but slowing down to dock. A shuttle from the Compound recorded live footage of the magnificent, spherical vessel. *Doesn't seem like a very aerodynamic shape*, Celine thought to herself. Once docked, the new guests would be shuttled over to the Compound for their first experience on Mars. To everyone's surprise and delight, an announcement was made over an intercom in the Commons explaining that the guests had chosen to sleep in their suites on the Fantasy, and thus would not be over-taxing the life support systems within the Compound.

Though Celine didn't find the exterior of the ship particularly luxurious, she was excited to meet the guests. Based on rumors, there would be a historian who had made outrageous claims about having Martian ancestors, a few investors who wanted to purchase land, a newlywed couple who desired an interplanetary honeymoon, and the Ballingers (a pop music duo/married couple that the twins were extremely excited to meet).

Anna once claimed that "anyone who's anyone" followed the Ballingers, though Celine had never heard of them. Celine pretended she was familiar with the pop group then later listened to a few of their songs via her Crystal—a pair of high-tech eyeglasses Alex had sent as a gift. It's a good thing she had the glasses because when she tried to find the Ballingers through Ugi, her normal source for research, Ugi went into error mode. Celine assumed Ugi wasn't able to retrieve any info about the singers because Mr. Rittenhouse, the colony's primary benefactor, didn't deem them important enough to be included in the expensive data sent from Earth to Mars.

However, in spite of his stinginess, he had updated some of the systems on behalf of the colonists. They had new food printers that gave their synthetic meals better flavor, consistency, and nutritional value. They also had a more efficient decontamination room, which meant colonists and guests alike would spend less time sanitizing upon entering the Compound premises. However, none of these developments would assist Celine in learning more about popular culture on Earth in the way that information on the Ballingers would have.

The ship docked, the guests from the Fantasy boarded the shuttles, and then they arrived on Mars. They spent ten minutes in the decontamination room, where they were vacuumed and disinfected. Then, they were considered safe and released into the Compound.

Admin, the head administrator of the Martian colony, stood by the entryway of the Commons alongside Asher (her equally composed assistant) and awaited the guests. Celine stood next to her parents. She held her dad's hand tightly.

"Everything will be okay," he said softly. "Your mother and my brother will be waiting for you when you reach Earth's moon."

Celine exhaled, then turned her attention to the guests. One by one, they entered. First was a gleeful tour director who radiated warmth and excitement. The director scanned the wary colonists who lined the walls.

"Greetings, everyone!" he exclaimed as he offered the group a wide, infectious smile. A handful of the colonists glanced at one another and smiled back at him. The director then turned his attention to Admin.

"Why, hello! You must be Admin and Asher!" he greeted, respectively offering them kind nods. "I'm Dr. Vee!"

"Ah, a doctor?" Admin enquired in surprise.

"Yes, indeed—doctor of intergalactic tourism! Pleased to make your acquaintance."

A few colonists chuckled, and Dr. Vee's eyes sparkled with joy. He twirled around grandly, revealing an iridescent radiation-proof cape. The colorful cape flared out and flowed with him as he spun. Most of the colonists either grinned, laughed, or offered a positive gesture somewhere in between. Then they all gave Dr. Vee a round of applause.

"Thank you, everyone!" Dr. Vee exclaimed as he bowed. "We're so delighted to be here on Mars. Now, let me introduce my esteemed visitors to your lovely Compound. It is a rather interesting set-up if I do say so myself."

More chuckles came from the colonists. Celine thought they seemed more relaxed by this point. There a brief moment of silence as a statuesque redhead with radiant brown skin and caramel-colored eyes stepped into the Commons. Venera was her name. She gave the group a friendly wave.

Chatter and smiles filled the room again. Celine thought she was beautiful, though something about her seemed eerily familiar.

Venera was followed by Mr. Abiola—an extremely tall man (at least two meters but perhaps taller) whose skin was as dark and rich as obsidian. He had one brown eye and one turquoise, and from Celine's perspective, he appeared to have two auras: two different shades of blue. *Strange.* Celine overheard a couple of colonists claim he was a bodyguard for one of the guests.

A happy, fit young couple held hands and blew kisses at the colonists as they made their way inside. These must be the newlyweds everyone had been chattering about, the Smiths, from a large block of land on Earth's North American continent called Texas. The Smiths seemed eager to integrate themselves into the Martian community and immediately walked up to a group of colonists, expressing their desire to get photos with the Martian moons, Phobos and Deimos, before their departure.

Several clean-cut investors considering purchasing lots in the lava tubes scurried inside as a cluster, alongside a couple of rather nerdy archaeologists planning to examine the planet's military base. They all offered nods and soft smiles as they walked in, but for the most part, they kept to themselves as they observed their new surroundings.

The Ballingers entered the Commons last. The twins, who rarely seemed to show emotion, looked as if they were about to burst with excitement. The Ballingers were a handsome couple from Earth's Canadian region. They both were of a bronze complexion, with chiseled bodies that they showed off in identical skintight metallic jumpsuits. Their dark mysterious eyes immediately lit up when they saw Celine.

After passing the entryway, they paused as if the crowd would take pictures. When no one did, Asher quickly whipped out a digital camera from his bag, crossed in front of them, and began snapping multiple photos. The Ballingers struck a variety of poses, angling their geometrically symmetric faces and well-toned bronzed bodies in different positions. Celine found herself imitating them, though she hadn't realized until she noticed the twins giggling and scoffing in her direction. Celine immediately stopped in embarrassment, but Mrs. Ballinger gave her a friendly wink. The twins' jaws dropped in envy.

"I'd like everyone's attention, please," announced Admin. "You'll be happy to learn that my dear cousin Mr. Rittenhouse has sponsored a banquet for all of us, prepared by the Fantasy's very own world-class chefs!"

Suddenly, an army of small Bots rolled into the Commons with trays of aromatic culinary dishes. Having been raised mostly on synthetic foods from the printer, Celine had never witnessed such elaborate plating techniques nor smelled such mouth-watering aromas. She noticed that many of the colonists beamed with delight, and even her dad licked his lips.

There were many dishes Celine had never heard of before such as short ribs, risotto, and caviar. She was most entranced by the decadent baked pasta made with milk from the large animals of Earth—Mac & Cheese.

Celine, her family, and the rest of the colonists ate as if they were famished. Coming up for air, Celine's dad admitted how much he had missed "real" meat. Everyone in the room, including the new arrivals, was in high spirits, eating—laughing, and chatting with one another. The meeting of the guests turned out better than anyone could've hoped.

Later that day, Celine sat alone in the infirmary after receiving her first dose of the antiradiation vaccine necessary for deep space travel. Asher entered the small medical office and announced that Dr. Vee would like to meet her.

"Huh?" Celine raised an eyebrow in confusion as if she hadn't fully processed the statement.

"Follow me, please." Asher turned to exit.

Celine's eyes widened as the information dawned on her, and she scrambled out of her seat and caught up with Asher.

After silently making their way through the halls of the Compound, Asher and Celine found Dr. Vee waiting in the Commons. Asher stopped near the doorway and then gestured for Celine to continue on. She timidly made her way to the center of the room.

"Celine! Such a pleasure to meet you," he said in admiration. "I trust you enjoyed the feast? The chefs are so incredibly talented, aren't they?"

"Oh, yes." Celine replied, eager to please but clearly a bit on edge.

"Wonderful." He beamed. Celine smiled back, unsure of what to say.

"Well I'm sure you're wondering why I've requested to see you, and the reason is simple," he stated. "I consider you to be a *very* special young lady, and I would love to have you on the tour with my guests."

Celine gasped slightly. Her eyes darted around the room, and her hands began to fidget as she struggled to come up with an appropriate response. Her mind was somehow racing and completely blank all at once.

"I've spoken with your parents and the Admin, and they've all given the green light. It's totally up to you, Celine."

"Why me, though?"

"Well, you are the first of your kind."

"My kind?"

"A Martian!" Dr. Vee burst into a fit of exuberant laughter. He composed himself slightly. "My guests have never met one." This comment tickled him even more and caused yet another giggle spell.

Celine didn't exactly understand the humor, but she liked the fact that Dr. Vee laughed so freely. She couldn't help but smile and chuckle.

"No pressure, but I did sort of promise my guests a firsthand experience with a real live Martian. What do you say, Celine?"

Celine could feel the nerves coursing through her body until she realized that she'd be up close and personal with the Ballingers. *The twins would be so impressed.*

"Okay, why not?" she responded. "I'll do it."

"Oh, fabulous! My guests will shuttle down first thing tomorrow morning. I've reserved the large glider for the tour, so meet us there at the 6th hour. Thank you."

The next morning, after having her usual breakfast of yellow-colored egg-and-bacon mush, Celine headed to Exit 16 to suit up. She checked her oxygen canister; it was 100% full—check. She reached into the front pouch of her suit and felt the package of emergency O2 pills—check. She pulled out her flat-water pack, made sure the cap was screwed on tight, then placed it back into the rear compartment of her suit—check. Celine had been learning how to prep her outerwear since she was 10 years old, and she knew the importance of getting everything right.

She keyed in the code to open the heavy airtight door, and it whooshed open, revealing the Martian terrain. As Celine stepped onto powdery red sand she inhaled deeply, taking in the unparalleled beauty of the butterscotch-colored morning sky. The glow from the sunlight shining through shades of rusty orange dust clung to her radiation suit.

"Air-lock 3, secure," she stated in an over-annunciated fashion, and the voice-automated door slid shut and sealed itself with a suctioning sound. Celine could see the glider in the distance and desperately wanted to sprint over to it, but she knew better. Outside of the Compound, running was a difficult feat, given the Martian gravity. She could potentially float too high and/or end up uncontrollably sailing right past the glider.

Now that would be embarrassing. She shook her head no and chuckled. Skipping at a nice, controlled pace made more sense.

All the guests were seated in the glider when Celine arrived. Most of them were dressed in simple suits like Celine's. However, both of the couples set themselves apart from the other guests. The Ballingers wore identical black and silver radiation suits and jeweled helmets, and the Smiths wore white ones with an intricate lace pattern. As Celine boarded, she smiled at each of the guests. Though a few of them weren't able to conceal their confusion, they all smiled back—except Mr. Abiola, who simply nodded in her direction with a straight face. There was an empty seat next to him and one next to Venera. Celine chose the latter and strapped herself in.

Dr. Vee looked as though he was struggling to keep a burning secret, on the verge of exploding with excitement. The guests, Celine included, patiently looked on in curiosity. Finally, Dr. Vee made the announcement that Celine was in fact the real live Martian who would be touring with them as promised; she'd be their go-to for any questions about Mars that he himself couldn't answer. Most guests' eyes widened with intrigue, and there was a wave of oohs, aahs, and "nice to meet you, Celine". After everyone's initial reactions, the guests took a moment to applaud Celine.

"Thank you," she responded shyly.

"No, thank *you*, Celine." Dr. Vee rapidly blew a stream of kisses her way before continuing. "We'll kick off the tour by flying over Olympus Mons, the largest volcano on Mars."

Very good choice, Celine thought to herself.

"In fact, it's the largest volcano in the universe." Dr. Vee paused to think. "Well, the largest in the Milky Way at least," he corrected.

Celine could hardly conceal her pride and excitement.

"After our view of the volcano, we'll head to Cydonia for a special surprise!" Dr. Vee's eyes gleamed with joy and genuine enthusiasm as he took his seat.

"Everyone comfortable?" he asked the group in a sing-songy tone.

"Yes, Dr. Vee," the guests said in unison before many dissolved into laughter.

"Well, up, up, and away we go then!" He nodded at the pilot. The pilot nodded back matter-of-factly, and the glider rose into the air and zoomed in the direction of the grand volcano.

Dr. Vee is an extraordinarily happy person, Celine thought as she surveyed him. *Even his aura is a richer than normal blue.* His joy was rather contagious, and Celine figured spending the day alongside him would lift her spirits.

Not to mention, because the gliders were generally only used by certain Newcomers getting to and from their workplaces (the caves and lava tubes primarily), Celine didn't fly often. Therefore, being on the glider was a real treat for her; she only wished she had someone her age to share it with.

As the unit flew above the rocky red terrain, the group acknowledged small dust devils in the distance in awe. Celine, however, was more focused on a large rock in the distance that vaguely resembled her lost dog, Puppy. Puppy was a wild dog that Celine had adopted when his mother was killed. He came from a long line of genetically-engineered dogs who lived on the planet long before the actual colonists arrived. His kind was bred to navigate survival amidst the fickle Martian temperatures (up to 21°C on summer days and as low as -140°C at night).

Puppy ran off a few months ago after only having been under Celine and her family's care for a matter of months. Celine's father told her that he'd probably left in search of others of his kind, though Celine had an inkling that the Newcomers had frightened him away. In an effort to console Celine, her mother sent a Robo-Pug with the colony's most recent cargo shipment from Earth. The toy had lavender-colored fur and short, stubby legs—nothing like Puppy. But it behaved more or less like a real pet, which Celine appreciated. She called him Puggie. It could bark, growl at people who weren't in its facial recognition database, and consumed energy packets in a similar fashion to how a real dog would gobble down its food. After its energizing "meal", Puggie's fur would re-fluff like new. All in all, Celine found the mechanical puppy to be a rather amusing and adorable companion. The downfall was that it needed to ingest one energy packet per month to function, and these packets represented a universal power source across the colony for most electronic devices. Admin soon requested that Celine turn the Robo-Pug off until the new power grid was completed because, as a result of the Newcomers' arrival, energy packets were reserved for specific usages, and powering pet-like toys, unfortunately, didn't constitute one of them. Celine sadly placed Puggie under her bunk, in the drawer next to her flute, but she knew a Robo-Pug would have never truly replaced Puppy anyhow. Whenever Celine got the chance to ride in a glider, as she did today, she'd be on the lookout for him.

"Wow! Look at the size of that thing!" exclaimed Mr. Ballinger as the group flew over Olympus Mons. "It's bigger than Mount Everest!"

"No, it can't be. I've seen Everest with my own two eyes," replied Mr. Smith.

Celine was a bit taken aback by Mr. Smith's assertion. She softly attempted to interject. "Um.. Well, like Dr. Vee said earlier, Olympus Mons is literally the biggest volcano in the—"

"Sorry, Mr. Smith, but you're wrong."

Mr. Smith whipped his head around to see who was insulting him, as Celine simultaneously looked back to see who had cut her off. It was one of the know-it-all investors, Mr. Monroe.

"Mount Everest, which sits at the China-Nepal border, is approximately 9 kilometers tall. On the contrary, the volcano you see here—Olympus Mons—is about 22 kilometers at its highest point."

"Why, thank you for the completely unsolicited information. What are you, a walking computer?" Mr. Smith sucked his teeth.

Dr. Vee quickly changed the subject. "We'll be arriving in Cydonia pretty soon! Get ready for another treat!"

Soon thereafter the glider landed, and the group arrived at a military base in Cydonia. As they deplaned, they were scanned by a humanoid security team, and to everyone's surprise (and some dismay) all recording devices were taken upon entry.

Celine had heard many different stories about the base. It had been on the planet a year prior to the colonists, and hardly anyone visited it, including herself. She knew that it was surrounded by electric fencing and guarded by mechanized soldiers who could turn organic matter to ash in a matter of seconds. She'd also heard a few colonists who'd visited claim that the base contained pyramids and sculptures which fabricated by the Rittenhouse Corporation to increase Mars' appeal to those back on Earth. Shortly after the group bypassed the security team, Celine realized that those colonists' statements were hardly more than claims.

The group walked into what seemed to be a mainly barren open space enclosed by metal fencing on the horizon. There were a few unmarked metal buildings along with a handful of hills built from rocks, which the archaeologists—"Marsologists" as they preferred to be called, given the nature of their work—appeared to be rummaging through. Dr. Vee explained that these hills were pyramids, but Celine wasn't all too impressed.

Looks like a big pile of dusty old rocks to me, she thought. There was also a large stone situated between two of the "pyramids" that seemed to be an ambiguous carving of a human head. Celine overheard Mr. Ballinger complimenting the wonderful work that the sculptors had done as he gestured toward it.

"Technically, this can be seen better from the air," Dr. Vee explained, "but we, unfortunately, weren't able to get clearance to fly above the military base. I'm so very sorry about that."

Dr. Vee proceeded to apologize profusely with an exaggerated frown on his face. The Marsologists interrupted his apology by rushing up to him, practically begging to take rock samples from the pyramids, but they, too, were denied. Dr. Vee put his face in his hands as if exasperated by having to refuse the guests their wishes. The Marsologists looked crestfallen. *What's the big deal?* Celine wondered. *They're just rocks.*

Later that afternoon, the fleet headed to the caves to see Alexander Lake, the subterranean lake that she and Alex had discovered on their journey together. While still en route, both Marsologists, Mrs. Smith, and the investors badgered Celine with questions surrounding the lake's discovery. Her answers were vague and short, as she didn't have much to say about an event that she'd worked to suppress in her memory. The guests looked displeased.

Celine noticed their expressions and said, "I may remember more when we get there; it's just been so long." She didn't actually believe this, but she hoped it'd get the guests off of her back for the time being.

They arrived at the caves right before the night fell and the cold set in. Celine remembered the Martian night temperatures were quite literally cold enough to freeze your eyeballs solid—a not-so-fun fun fact Ugi had taught her. Just reflecting on it made Celine shiver and hug herself for warmth. However, luckily for the group (and their eyeballs), the caves were warm and insulated.

The Smiths stood posed at the cave's entrance while one of several miniature Bots that'd been released from the glider— referred to as "Valets"—took an array of stunning photos with the dusk sky in the background. The newlyweds got the shots they came to Mars for— both of Mars' moons in the background, and, best of all, Earth, which appeared as a blue dot in the darkening sky. They were elated.

The Valets began setting up tents inside the empty cavern, which was the largest cave near the southern end of the lake, only a few miles from the water filtration plant. Celine's heart sank as Dr. Vee assured the group that their one-night stay in the cave was completely authorized and safe, and he guided everyone one by one to their assigned tents.

While this had been an exciting day for her, she had no idea she'd be spending the night in a cave let alone the one where the bulk of her past trauma had occurred. Had she known, she wouldn't have joined the tour. Celine plopped down onto the twin-sized foam mattress pad designated as her sleeping space and let out a disgruntled sigh. Her tentmate, Venera, interrupted her thoughts.

"I really expected more from this planet," Venera glumly said to herself as she stared into the distance.

Celine sat up to lay eyes on Venera and was astonished by her striking profile. The way the dim light from the cave hit her red hair was an exquisite sight. Celine snapped out of her brief daze and cleared her throat. "What were you expecting?"

Venera shrugged her shoulders. "I don't really feel like talking about it."

"Oh. I-I'm sorry… I-I just… I-I—"

"Sorry. It's been a long day."

Celine gulped, then obliged by shutting her mouth and shifting her gaze away from Venera. Blood rushed to her cheeks as the embarrassment from stuttering started to set in. *Why are people from Earth so complicated?* She lightly scoffed at the confusing nature of the interaction, but she quickly stifled it into a cough when she realized she might potentially offend Venera. *I just know I won't fit in on Earth.*

Celine looked across the cavern at the other tents and occupants. Most were already tucked into bed. She gave a fake yawn as she unfolded the thick blanket provided at the edge of the mattress pad and laid it across her body. She nestled into her pillow and layed, facing the tent wall.

Hours passed.

Celine couldn't fall asleep. Though the cave's appearance had changed quite a bit since she and Alex were there, she couldn't shake the sense of anxiety she felt being back. The night lighting that the Newcomers had installed somehow amplified how unsettling it all was. The only thing that would allow Celine to make it through the night was knowing that they'd be leaving the caves at sunrise. Too bad she had no way of telling the hour. There were no clocks to be found, and Celine's sense of time had completely collapsed the moment the sunset. *This is going to be a long night.*

CHAPTER 3

MARTIAN CAVES ARE NOT SAFE

Morning eventually came, although Celine, as expected, did not sleep. She heard some muffled chatter in the distance and decided to peer outside the tent. To her right was the cave entryway, and to her left was Mr. Abiola who was faintly illuminated by the morning light. He was conversing with someone deep inside the cave near the red mud puddles, though his large size obscured Celine's view of whomever he was speaking to. Celine found it odd that one would venture so deeply into the cavern without knowing what dangers might be lurking about.

Venera yawned, which startled Celine back inside the tent. Celine sat motionless on her sleeping pad as Venera stretched.

"Good morning," Venera said to Celine as she rubbed her eyes.

"Hi there. I mean, good morning," Celine responded nervously.

She was eager to make a good impression. Celine's awkwardness was apparent, but her youthful charm made Venera grin.

"How'd you sleep?" she asked Celine.

"Not good. I don't like this place at night."

Venera offered Celine an empathetic frown to illustrate her pity, as one might do to a child who says they had a bad dream. She then shifted her focus to tidying up her sleeping area. As Venera folded her bed sheets and primped, Celine quietly shuffled back over to the opening of the tent and continued to watch Mr. Abiola. He appeared to be reaching out for something to the right of him, but nothing was there.

Suddenly, Celine felt a surge of fear and adrenaline coursing through her body as memories of the traumatic, life-threatening, hallucination-filled experiences in the caves came rushing back in full force.

"We have to leave this place!' Celine yelled as she jolted up and scrambled to put on her radiation suit. "We have to leave this place *now!*"

"Celine, calm down. What's the matter?" Venera hurried over to the tent opening and peered down the path Celine had been looking toward. Her eyes followed Mr. Abiola as he headed back toward the camp, though she retreated inside the tent before it became blatantly obvious that she was staring.

Meanwhile, Celine quickly fastened her suit and secured her helmet. She snatched down the zipper of the tent opening, widening it so that she could step through more easily. In her haste, however, Celine still tripped out onto the cave floor as she attempted to squeeze past Venera. She hobbled to her feet and turned around to face her tentmate, who was completely taken aback as she watched the scene play out.

"I'll be waiting in the glider," Celine said to Venera as she scurried away.

Dr. Vee emerged from his tent fully dressed, looking to gauge the source of the commotion. Celine noticed him but was not willing to wait for his questions and continued on her way. Dr. Vee animatedly grabbed his chest and took a step backward to express the shock he felt as Celine rushed past him without saying a word.

"Goodness gracious, what happened?" Dr. Vee asked Venera.

"I'm not sure… Celine was looking down there," Venera pointed toward the darker section of the cave, "and she said we needed to get out right now. She was frantic."

Dr. Vee raised an eyebrow as he stared into the dark, abyss-like part of the cave. His eyes slowly widened.

"Well, my wonderful guests, it's time to rise and shine!" he shouted across the cavern as he fastened his helmet. "I'll be waiting in the glider," he said as he ran after Celine.

"Hurry, everyone," Dr. Vee yelled back at the guests from the cave entryway. "Don't get left behind!"

He scampered off.

Everyone remaining in the caves began suiting up as quickly as they could.

"What's the hurry?" Mr. Abiola asked the group.

"Who knows?" Mr. Smith responded from a few tents over. "That Vee fellow sure is one excitable guy."

"I know, right?" Mrs. Smith responded, holding on to her husband's arm for balance as she put her shoes on. "I love him!"

The couple grinned at each other, clearly relishing all of the quirks of their honeymoon.

"Y'all heard the man," Mr. Smith shouted. "Better hurry before you get left behind!" He chuckled lightheartedly then paused for a moment. "He better not dare," he murmured as he helped fasten Mrs. Smith's helmet.

A Valet quickly zoomed in between the Smiths, who both jumped out of its way. All of the other Valets began moving about as well, quickly breaking down, sanitizing, and repacking the tents and floor coverings. Once all of the guests were geared up, they headed toward the exit as a collective unit.

On the glider, Dr. Vee questioned Celine about why they had to leave the cave so quickly.

"Mr. Abiola was acting weird," she said.

"Is that all? He's a strange guy… Oh my goodness," Dr. Vee let out a moan. "We got everyone in a rush for nothing?!"

Celine stayed silent. She would rather let Dr. Vee think they rushed out for no reason than get into the intricacies of why Mr. Abiola's behavior frightened her to her core.

The guests began boarding the glider and taking their seats.

"Are you all right?" Venera asked Celine as she took the seat next to her.

"I'm fine. Hopefully, we all are," she said as she glanced over at Mr. Abiola, fixing her gaze on his bizarre yet mesmerizing two-toned eyes. Before she knew it, the two of them were locked in a deep stare.

"I'm fine, too. Thank you, Celine," he said in response to her previous statement. He offered a rather cold, closed-lip smile before breaking eye contact and turning his head toward the window, watching the view as the glider zoomed away.

The group's final stop on the tour was the Rover Graveyard Museum. The group saw the first lander, Mars 3. Celine learned that it had come from a country on Earth that no longer existed—The Soviet Union. It landed in 1973 and failed to transmit any photos back to Earth. They also came across the Zhurong rover that landed in 2021, which came from China (another country on Earth that Celine was only vaguely familiar with). Then Dr. Vee led them to a designated area of rovers from the United States, the place where Celine's mother and father had spent their childhoods. The landers Vikings 1 and 2 arrived in 1976, and the Sojourner, the Spirit, Opportunity, Curiosity, and the Perseverance were all sent to Mars starting in the late 20th century. Celine thought the rovers looked like a fleet of giant mechanical insects with freakishly long, motionless legs—although it sent chills down her spine, it was definitely a sight to see.

After a two-day-long journey, the team finally returned to the Compound. Everyone was exhausted. The guests decided they would take an early shuttle ride back up to the Fantasy. They all thanked Celine for touring with them then headed to Airlock 3 where they waited to be escorted back to their luxury quarters.

Celine made her way to Airlock 16, which offered a shortcut to her and her parents' quarters. Walking through the Commons, she was relieved that she didn't run into any of the other teens. Prior to the excursion, Celine assumed that the twins would find her up-close-and-personal encounter with the Ballingers—the most famous singers on Earth—impressive and interesting. However, in her drained, post-tour state, Celine realized she'd have no idea how to navigate the confrontation.

She proceeded to her parents' quarters. Her stepmom wasn't there but her dad was at his desk, deeply engaged in a research project. When Celine entered, he stopped right away and greeted her with a warm smile. Celine had taken notice that her father had been quick to put his work aside for her lately. On one hand, she was happy that her dad was being more attentive than normal, but it saddened her to think that perhaps he was doing it because she wouldn't see him for nearly two years once she departed for Earth.

"How was the tour?" he asked as he logged out of his computer.

"It was a lot of fun!" she exclaimed with both genuine excitement and noticeable fatigue. She proceeded to tell him about all of the views and destinations, leaving out the experience in the cave earlier that morning.

Mr. Red Cloud beamed as his daughter recounted her experiences. His smile began to melt away as he steered the conversation elsewhere.

"And how are you feeling about the voyage next week? Now that you've spent some time with your travel companions, are you a little more comfortable with the idea?"

Celine's soft smile faded as well. "I'll be fine, Dad," she responded unconvincingly. She stared back at her dad, who said nothing, allowing her time to express her true thoughts. Celine bit her lower lip.

"I'm going to miss you, Dad... and I'm going to miss Hannah... and my baby brother... He'll already be two when I get back!" Celine let out a distressed sigh as her eyes started to get a bit misty.

"No tears, Celine," Mr. Red Cloud responded as he placed a comforting hand on her shoulder. "Earth is a beautiful place— lots of colorful plants, tons of animals, the latest technologies...You'll love it."

"Yeah, maybe. But…"

"But what?"

Celine rubbed her hands together nervously as she lowered her head. "I don't make friends that easily."

Her father gently lifted her chin.

"Your grandmother always used to say, 'You don't make friends, you find your tribe.' Understand?"

"Yeah, I guess," she shrugged.

Celine knew that she and her father were part of the Cherokee tribe, but she'd never met anyone else who was—perhaps she'd have more luck down on Earth.

"Now listen," her father continued, deepening his voice in an authoritative manner. "Make sure you follow all of the safety protocols. Don't assume anything. Ask questions."

Celine nodded affirmatively.

"Your uncle will meet you at Artemis," Mr. Red Cloud continued. "I've transferred his Com number to ours, and he also has the main number of the ship. As soon as you're assigned an extension, call me and I'll liaise."

Celine made an 'OK' hand gesture.

"And by the way, Celine…" He paused in contemplation. "I want you to have fun, but please be safe. Don't let anyone talk you into doing anything you'll regret."

Celine knew he was referring to her and the twins' shenanigan with the food printer.

"Don't worry, I'll make you proud," she said as she reached for her father and hugged him tightly. "Love you, Dad."

"Love you, too. I'll miss you."

The week sped by, and in the blink of an eye, it was time for Celine to take the shuttle up to The Fantasy. Celine approached the boarding area with her dad and stepmom, carrying one backpack that held all of her belongings. She couldn't help but notice that Anna and Nina, on the other hand, carried two each, as did their mother who wasn't even heading back to Earth yet. Celine watched Mando shake his head in disapproval. Both of Mando's parents shot reprimanding glares at him. He sucked his teeth in defeat. Mr. Red Cloud caught the interaction and chuckled to himself.

"Here, let me help you," Mr. Red Cloud said to the twins' mother as he took the bedazzled duffle bags from her arms.

"Oh, thank you," she said with a sigh of relief. "My girls just have so much stuff."

The teens and their parents boarded the shuttle and milled around for a while until an authoritative computerized voice emitted from the intercom.

"Be seated."

Once everyone took their seats, automated padded enclosures activated and strapped them in. Soon thereafter, the shuttle revved up and lifted off.

During takeoff, Celine didn't find the ride too uncomfortable, though she was definitely aware of how confining the padded straps were. As the shuttle picked up speed, however, she felt as though a strong force was trying to drive her small frame through the seat. The intensity of the air pulled her cheeks backward well beyond the point of comfort. The force made her face—and everyone else's—look distorted. This was nothing like her cruise in the glider.

If this is what deep space travel is like, she thought, *this three-month trek to Earth is going to be the hardest thing I've ever done.*

Fortunately, the painful ride didn't last very long, and they soon docked next to the Fantasy.

Once they were released from their seats, a large armlike appendage floated from a disk on the ceiling and attached itself to the shuttle door. The shuttle door slid open, and the group composed themselves before stepping into what looked like a white marble hall, the sanitizing room.

Though this room didn't serve a particularly luxurious purpose, it had a posh feel to it nonetheless. Being in this room re-emphasized the feeling that Celine was about to step into a totally different world than the one she'd been raised in.

"Please remain still," a friendly feminine voice said via a surround-sound system.

Crevices in the wall and ceiling spread apart, and the soft humming sound of a vacuum began. In a matter of seconds, every grain of the soft Martian dust in the vicinity was whisked away.

"Now *this* is the latest technology," Nina said as she gave Celine the side eye.

Celine was hit with a burst of embarrassment as she recalled the noisy vacuum they had in the sanitation room back at the Compound.

"Please close your eyes," the female voice said as the vacuum openings resealed themselves.

The all-white room suddenly emitted a blue light, which not only killed any bacteria and viruses but also created an incredibly tranquil ambiance. After a few moments, the blue light turned off and a door, which was designed to look like another wall, slipped open, revealing a unisex dressing room area. Loose-fitting white tops and pants, one-size-fits-all, lay folded neatly on marble countertops. Everyone grabbed their outfits and headed into stalls. Hannah couldn't stop marveling at what a great idea it was to change into fresh clothes after the sanitizing process.

Celine was more impressed with the slippers. They were so soft and cushy, offering her feet a sensation they'd never experienced. Not only that but now she wouldn't have to wear her ugly boots. *Bless!* From inside her stall, Celine heard her father tell Mando that these slippers reminded him of his old walking shoes back on Earth.

Once everyone was dressed and ready, the group transitioned into a waiting area in front of a wide ornate door.

"You may now enter the Commons," the voice on the speaker announced after a few moments. The door opened inward into the ship, and the group stepped into a common area that reminded Celine of the ballrooms she'd seen in movies. There was an abundance of decor made of crystal, including elaborately designed chandeliers. The space also featured an array of abstract art pieces both hanging and standing, all of which looked like they belonged in a contemporary art museum. The small areas of the walls that weren't covered with mirrors were painted a pale blue color that had a calming effect, not unlike the blue light in the sanitizing room.

There were fluffy white chairs and round silver tables scattered about. It was obvious that the Commons on this ship was not designed purely for work and functionality like the Commons back at the Compound was. In fact, this Commons looked like a party venue, and Celine was astonished by the size, considering the small number of people that'd be traveling on the ship.

Dr. Vee entered the room, followed by all of the original guests who were dressed in similar white outfits.

"Greetings, new travelers," he projected cheerfully across the Commons. "And beloved dinner guests," he interjected as he gestured toward the teens' parents. "Welcome aboard the Fantasy! It's time to party!"

Suddenly, a holographic band of twelve members appeared on a round stage in the center of the room and started playing lo-fi jazz tunes. Shortly thereafter a team of six Valets glided in, carrying trays of very interesting-smelling foods.

"Valets over here," Dr. Vee called out, and three of the Bots floated toward the group of new arrivals.

"Enjoy the food," Dr. Vee exclaimed. "These appetizers should hold you over until they've finished up in the Meat Lab."

"What are appetizers?" Celine asked her dad. "And what's a meat lab?"

Mr. Red Cloud's mouth was too full to answer. He was picking food off the tray with a glee in his eyes that Celine had rarely seen.

"Cream cheese, smoked salmon, cucumbers… I'll try one of each," he said.

"Dad," Celine whined.

"What?" he responded with a mouth stuffed full of delicacies.

Celine noticed a couple particles of food fly out of his mouth when he answered, and her stomach turned. "Never mind."

She took a few pastries from one of the trays and held them in her palm before popping a whole one into her mouth. The pastry practically melted on her tongue. She didn't know foods could have such exquisite textures.

The twins cackled amongst themselves as they watched Celine. Celine smiled at them, hoping desperately that it'd ease the awkwardness.

As the Valet slid over to the twins, they each delicately grabbed one pastry from the tray and took a tiny bite before smiling condescendingly at Celine.

Celine's smile disappeared. *Oh, rations!* She rushed over to try and put the food back onto the tray, but the Bot flew out of her reach.

"Unsanitary," they heard the bot say as it sped off.

Anna and Nina nearly choked on their tiny bites of pastry and laughed until they both had tears running down their cheeks. Celine stood uncomfortably in silence.

"So sorry. Excuse my manners," Anna said to Celine before walking off to mingle with the other guests. Nina followed, still laughing and wiping the tears from her eyes.

Celine turned to Mando, who was enjoying a plate of cucumbers and salmon cakes within earshot of Celine and the twins' interaction.

"I did something stupid, didn't I?"

"Not exactly. But technically, it's polite to only take one hors d'oeuvre until everyone else has a chance to get one."

"Take one what?"

"Hors d'oeuvre. Like, an appetizer."

Celine looked back at Mando with a blank stare.

"A piece of food," he responded with a light-hearted eye roll.

"Oh, I see." Celine had a brief moment of realization, but confusion quickly washed over her face again. She then whipped her head around to look at her dad, who had gobbled down several pieces of practically *everything* before anyone even got a good look at what was being served.

"Well, girls usually get just one piece of food and then nibble on it. It's to be *extra* polite, I guess," Mando replied as the two watched Mr. Red Cloud continue to gorge himself.

"Girls… nibble?" Celine cocked her head to the side in utter bewilderment, as if she were a confused puppy who'd just heard an unfamiliar sound in the distance.

"Yes, girls nibble." Mando playfully demonstrated with his salmon puff before joining the twins and leaving Celine to fend for herself.

Celine clammed up when she thought about the fact that she'd been on the ship for less than an hour, yet had already made a handful of mistakes. She closed her eyes and took a deep breath. She reminded herself that mistakes led to learning and growth, and nothing was going to stop her from learning the ways of Earth's teenagers and, of course, winning the twins' friendship in the process. As she opened her eyes, feeling refreshed and reassured, she noticed the twins and Mando staring at her. The twins were chuckling, and Mando looked on with a straight face before initiating a conversation with Nina to change the subject.

Celine grunted in frustration before defeatedly making her way over to her dad and Hannah, who were chatting and snacking at one of the tables.

After a while of waiting, two tables of food were wheeled into the Commons by the two head chefs. The foods were enclosed in glass, but Celine could still smell the flavorful aromas emitting from the steam vents beneath the tables. There was a "cold table" full of raw vegetables and fruits, and a "hot table" with different types of meats and starchy dishes. At the front of each table was a sanitizing station where guests would stick their hands inside a metal box radiating blue-light until a beep indicated that they were germ-free.

As Celine gazed at all of the food options, she was amazed at how colorful and vibrant the spread was. "This is real food—not synthetic," her father had said. Celine had been eating so-called synthetic food her entire life and wondered why exactly it didn't qualify as "real".

Celine wanted to try everything, but she remembered what Mando had said about taking only one food item until everyone had an opportunity to grab some. She ultimately chose a pasta dish with tomato sauce that the majority of guests already seemed to have on their plates. She then started to make her way back to the table to sit with her parents.

As she maneuvered through the Commons, she noticed that Mr. Abiola was sitting alone, but he had two plates of food on his table and appeared to be eating from both.

Girls nibble, Celine remembered, though she gazed longingly at the smorgasbord of delicious food back on the hot and cold tables. She took a seat and daintily started to pick at her pasta, observing all her traveling companions as she nibbled. Some had very kind faces, welcoming energy; others were difficult to read.

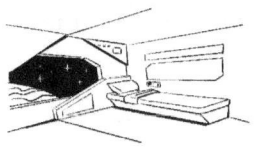

CHAPTER 4

IS THIS WHERE WE SLEEP?

All the guests left the Commons area and headed for their suites. All except Celine, Mando, Anna, and Nina, none of whom had been assigned one. Dr. Vee informed the teens that they would be traveling "economy class" and proceeded to guide them down to the sleeping hall where most of the ship's employees slept.

After walking the length of the ship, they arrived at the sleeping hall: a large marble hallway where the walls were embedded with rows of convex glass enclosures. Dr. Vee called them sleeping Pods. Inside the Pods were beds, only slightly larger than the bunk Celine slept in back on Mars.

"I don't usually have people your age on my trips," Dr. Vee told the group. "Deep space can be a dangerous place—far too dangerous for children in my opinion. But I'm bringing you home as a favor to your lovely parents, so don't get into any trouble," he explained, looking directly at Anna and Nina during the latter part of his statement.

Celine knew her parents were saving up towards furnishing their new home and the expenses for her new baby brother. She had been wondering how they were able to afford such an expensive trip to Earth, so she was relieved to learn they didn't have to pay.

"I'm sorry, but we only have three Pods available: 2, 3, and 4," Dr. Vee continued. "Take your pick. You should all get some rest, and you're encouraged to sleep through our departure at 3:24 am."

Anna opened her mouth to speak, but before she could make a sound, Dr. Vee announced, "And please save any questions, comments, or concerns for tomorrow. I'm currently running on E. I'll see you all in the morning. Sweet dreams!"

And with that, Dr. Vee exited the sleeping hall and headed for his suite alongside the paying guests.

"This is so kind of Dr. Vee to do this as a favor for our parents," Celine said, breaking the group's silence.

"Are you kidding? I thought we'd have luxury suites," groaned Nina. "Disappointing!"

In frustration, she kicked the Pod she was standing next to. To everyone's surprise, the orb-like plexiglass door whistled open and a neatly made bed rose. Nina dove into the chamber, and Anna plopped onto the bed next to her sister.

"I guess they expect us to share, huh?" Anna sighed.

The twins looked at each other and squinched their faces in unison.

"It won't be that bad," Mando reassured them. He had come to Mars on a luxury spaceship similar to The Fantasy and slept in a sleeping hall much like this one.

"We'll get to use all the other amenities and let me tell you—the food is great!"

Anna perked up, but Nina pouted. Nina popped out of the Pod and quickly examined the neighboring sleeping chambers.

"We'll take this Pod," she said, returning to the one her sister was on. "It looks the biggest." She started fiddling with the keypad next to Pod 2, trying to figure out how to set up its privacy code.

Mando chuckled. "They're all the same size, Nina."

Celine decided on Pod 3 next to the twins, and Mando went across the hall and began inputting his privacy code into Pod 4's keypad.

After setting up their privacy code, Nina collapsed back onto the bed and adjusted herself to a comfortable sleeping position, practically crushing her sister with her body weight while doing so. Anna grumbled angrily as she hoisted Nina to the other side of the bed.

"How is this going to work?" Anna barked.

"You can sleep behind me, next to the wall," Nina responded with a mischievous grin. Anna scoffed in sisterly disgust.

Celine took off her boots and climbed into her Pod. The spherical glass secured itself, enclosing her inside, and she immediately felt heat circulating throughout. The mattress was warm and bouncy. Her stiff bunk back at the Compound paled in comparison to this "economy" Pod. Celine adjusted the two fluffy pillows in the Pod to her liking and wrapped herself in the blanket. She stretched out and wiggled her toes, enjoying the feel of the soft material around her feet.

"Now *this* is luxurious," she whispered.

Later that night, Celine was awakened by kicking against her wall—the one adjacent to the twins' sleeping area. She heard Nina yell at Anna to stop snoring, which Anna emphatically denied before accusing Nina of being the snorer. After several minutes of back-and-forth, the twins' Pod went silent as they drifted to sleep again. Celine, however, couldn't fall back asleep. She lay on her side, facing the outer glass wall of her Pod.

Every sound on the ship seemed heightened. She could hear the clicking sounds of the planetary clock, even though it was situated all the way out in the main hall. She heard Mando, whose Pod was across the hall from hers, rip a fart. But worse than that, she could hear both twins snoring.

Suddenly, Celine heard a noise that she couldn't quite identify. It sounded like someone was scurrying through the main hall. She wondered who would be out of their bedroom at this hour. The sound was getting closer, and it seemed to stop right at the entrance of the sleeping hall. Though her eyes were half-closed, Celine saw a flare of blue light that reminded her of the auras she had always seen around the colonists. It was like a blue shadow of a human. She waited for a person to move into the light, but the shadow seemed to have a life of its own. It was like nothing she had seen before. The human-esque ball of light charged toward Celine's Pod, and she quickly closed her eyes. It paused there for a few seconds. She could hear breathing, but she dared not open her eyes. Then, all of a sudden, it was quiet. Celine waited and listened for what felt like hours. Finally, she opened her eyes, and the blue shadow was gone. She rolled over onto her back and wrapped her arms around her chest.

Was that a dream? Wait… It has to be past 3:24—maybe I'm hallucinating.

Celine stared at the ceiling of her Pod and bit her lower lip. A good night's sleep unfortunately would not be on her agenda for the night. Realizing that the light of day would never come out in deep space, she anxiously awaited the artificial-morning simulation in hopes that it'd offer her some semblance of safety.

Hours later, after only a few fretful moments of sleep, Celine's bloodshot eyes snapped open as the ceiling lights brightened above her and strange chirping sounds filled her Pod. Across the hall, Mando was awake and putting on his slippers. Celine waved at him, then tapped on the release button imprinted on the Pod wall to open her door.

"You look terrible," Mando said as she approached him.

Celine shifted uncomfortably and began frantically fixing her hair. She looked over at the twins' Pod and noticed their absence, and all the insecurity left her body. She stopped primping and let out an aggressive yawn.

"I just didn't sleep well."

"Oh, that makes sense! Was the air too warm or was the bed too soft?" he joked.

Celine wanted to tell him she had seen a shadow in the middle of the night that looked like a full-blown human aura, but she was quite sure he'd have no idea what she was talking about. Not only that, but Celine's parents, Dr. Baylor, and Alex were the only ones who knew about her vision capabilities when it came to picking up light waves. Granted, a few colonists suspected that she was different, but they had no proof. For the time being, she wanted to keep it that way.

"The twins snored all night," she responded, suppressing her true concerns.

A loudspeaker announcement interrupted her lie. *Thank goodness.* It was Dr. Vee, as jovial as ever.

"Good morning, guests!"

His voice had such a joyful intonation, it sounded like he was on the verge of singing. "Breakfast will be served shortly."

Almost as if on cue, a variety of breakfast food fragrances blasted throughout the ship.

"Do you smell that?" Mando asked Celine as he inhaled deeply. "Bacon, scrambled eggs with cheese, and cinnamon rolls! Dr. Vee definitely has a way of making people do what he wants. I'm heading up!"

Celine joined him. On their way to the Commons, the teens passed four Valets that were heading in the direction of the sleeping hall and carrying their belongings. Mando noticed Celine backtrack toward the Bots but he assured her that they knew where to put her backpack, and she caught back up with him. They continued onward.

"Those things know the entire ship inside and out. It's part of their programming," he said reassuringly. "They're literally made to help us."

The Bots back on Mars were not personable whatsoever. They had tasks to do, carrying heavy construction materials, building more habitats, etc. For Celine, having a bot to cater to her specific needs seemed a bit excessive, though she noticed it didn't seem to bother Mando or anyone else on the Fantasy.

When they passed the ship's flower garden, Celine heard that strange chirping sound that had awakened her.

"Do you hear that?" she said.

"What?"

"That horrible *cheeping* thing?"

"They're bird sounds. You've never heard a bird before?!" Mando asked, completely astonished.

Celine shook her head.

"Not even in a science lesson or anything?" Mando continued in amazement.

"Thankfully, no."

"A lot of people actually like the sound of birds. Calming, ya know?"

"Well, I heard it this morning and thought my Pod was infested with insects. It was super creepy."

Mando burst into laughter. "Let your Valet know," he said, attempting to compose himself. "It'll help you pick another wake-up call."

"I definitely will."

"On Earth, there are birds everywhere. Some of them even caw!" Mando jested, imitating a crow.

"Ah, of course, there are," Celine grunted. "One more thing to add to my never-ending list of things to learn before we get to Earth."

"Don't worry. I got your back." He gave Celine a pat on her shoulder blade.

She had never heard that expression and had no idea what he meant, but she thanked him, nevertheless.

When they arrived at the Commons, most of the guests were sitting in plush chairs at small, intimate tables, enjoying an array of foods and drinks. The hologram band played soft, soothing background tunes. Celine noticed all the guests had warm blue auras, except Mr. Abiola who appeared to have two auras: each a different shade of blue, neither one of them on par with the hue of the other guests.

"Why are you staring at everyone?" Mando asked.

"Oh. I didn't realize I was," she said nonchalantly, hoping to downplay her actions.

As Celine hypothesized about the potential meanings behind a double aura, she noticed the blue shadow again. It appeared to have peeled away from Mr. Abiola and moved toward the breakfast carts. She let out a light gasp, and Mr. Abiola, as if in response, immediately got up and walked toward the pastry table, obscuring Celine's view of the blue shadow. He took a plate of pastries from the table and headed back toward the entrance. When he exited the Commons, Celine scanned the room. It appeared as though the blue shadow had left him.

"Did you see that?" Celine impulsively asked Mando, who had but a few drops of his green smoothie left after already gobbling down a plate of pancakes, scrambled eggs, and bacon.

"See what?" he queried as he licked syrup from his fingers.

Celine realized she had spoken too quickly. *Of course, he didn't see it. He can't.*

"Never mind. I'll be back," she responded as she headed to the hall, hopeful for a better look at Mr. Abiola and the shadow.

"Don't touch my food!" she called out to Mando as she speed-walked to the hall.

Celine reached the hall and looked up and down in both directions. Neither Mr. Abiola nor the shadow was anywhere to be found.

Dejectedly she returned to the table in the Commons, and at this point her breakfast was cold. Nonetheless, she ate it without thinking twice. Food was never wasted in the Compound.

"You know you could have gotten another plate of hot food if you wanted."

"I know. I'm okay, though."

"You're not acting like it," Mando responded, observing Celine's glum mannerisms. "The first time I went into deep space, I got really sick. I had headaches, intense stomach aches... Some people even hallucinate—it's fine if you're a little out of orbit.. Get it? 'Orbit'?"

"Yeah, I get it," Celine replied letting out a half-hearted chuckle, although she wasn't amused. "I'm fine," she continued, even though she felt entirely discombobulated.

"Did you find what you were looking for?"

Celine twisted uncomfortably in her chair. She suddenly had a heavy feeling in her stomach, as if her breakfast was about to make its way back up.

Just in the nick of time, the twins made their way into the Commons. They always walked into a room as if they were strutting on a fashion runway, and Celine was relieved that Mando noticed them right away. Her stomach was feeling queasy, and any more talk about what she may or may not have seen would've accelerated that feeling without a doubt.

"Come join us," he called out and waved them over.

Before the twins could join them, a blaring alarm began to sound throughout the ship. Suddenly, Dr. Vee ran into the Commons. "Everyone, get to the nearest water room. Stat!"

"Water room? What's he talking about?" Mando asked Celine, flustered.

"The garden! Let's go!" Celine yelled back to him as she hurried away from the table, past the twins, and into the garden area. Mando and the twins followed. The doors to the garden shut behind them, and the radiation shades came down to cover the large windows that allowed the passengers to look out at the real stars during the ship's artificial night-time simulations.

All of a sudden, Anna tapped Celine on the shoulder.

"How did you know we were supposed to come in here?" she asked Celine suspiciously.

"Oh, I just read the safety manual," she said sheepishly. "Did you?"

Anna held back a giggle. "Good to know," she responded as she headed toward her sister and Mando, avoiding Celine's question.

After a few moments, Dr. Vee made an announcement.

"This was a safety drill. You may resume your affairs."

"I guess we probably all should go over the safety manual then," Celine overheard Mando say in conversation with the girls.

Nina laughed and batted her long eyelashes. For the first time, Celine noticed that Nina's left eye released fewer heat waves than the right one. In fact, her left eye seemed quite different in a lot of respects. It moved differently—almost machine-like. Unlike everyone else, Celine could easily tell the twins apart, particularly because Nina was slightly smaller and had a distorted, jagged aura around her. Occasionally it was blue in hue like everyone else's, but most often—as it was at this moment—it was red, which Celine discovered correlated to some degree of frustration and/or rage. Anna, on the other hand, almost always had a light blue aura that was smooth around the edges. The twins may be identical, but they surely processed their emotions differently, and Celine could see it. Plus, now with this full awareness, Celine wondered if the difference in Nina's aura had anything to do with her left eye.

The protective window shades in the garden arose post-drill, and Celine noticed a cylinder-shaped asteroid in the distance that seemed to be headed toward Mars from the belt. For a split second, she felt an influx of worry, but it quickly dissipated as she stared at the asteroid and reminded herself that it didn't present any kind of threat to her loved ones. In ancient times, asteroids used to create small craters on the planet every other day, but thanks to the Mars Space Force—the planet's military team—they'd destroy any asteroid heading their way with a Particle Disruptor.

Finally, the Fantasy had moved far enough into space for her to see the entire Red Planet far in the distance. She noticed the cloudlike slithers of frozen carbon dioxide at each of the planet's poles. It was truly magnificent. Her father had reminded her that Earth was also quite beautiful from outer space but she found that difficult to believe, especially in comparison to her home planet.

She knew that the invisible forces of gravity and inertia allowed the planets to stay in their orbits around the sun, but from this view her home world seemed like a large spinning ball moving on its own through an expansive sea of blackness. It seemed so fragile. She felt an ache in her chest as she observed her home from such a distance.

"I miss you already," she whispered longingly.

Celine was suddenly pulled out of her daze when she heard the twins approaching. She whipped around to face them.

"Wow, you really read the entire safety manual? All 23 pages?" Nina asked with an impish grin on her face.

"Of course." *Reading twenty-three pages is nothing.*

After a slight pause to try and conceal their amusement, the twins burst into laughter.

What is so funny? Why am I always the butt of their jokes?

Celine was proud of herself for knowing exactly what to do in the case of an emergency, and she stood there awkwardly, hoping to eventually gain some insight into what the girls were cackling at.

"You always know what to say to make us laugh," Anna finally said.

Celine smiled with closed lips. She often referred to Anna as the "good twin", since she usually had something positive to say. Nonetheless, both twins were very mischievous, and Celine knew that wasn't a genuine compliment. It was also, quite frankly, the furthest thing from the truth.

"I gotta go," she responded as she awkwardly shuffled out of the garden.

The next day, the teens were scheduled for their first world-history class. On Mars, Celine's lessons were always done alone or with Ugi, so she was apprehensive about her first in-class experience with other human beings.

She entered the classroom, which was futuristic and sleek though certainly not designed for young students. She took a seat at one of the large desks upfront. Shortly after, the twins and Mando made their way into the room, engaged in robust conversation as they took their seats.

The ship's media specialist doubled as their instructor. When she walked in, the room fell silent. She was dressed in all-black, which gave her a sophisticated aesthetic appearance, though her mannerisms were very loose and relaxed. After settling into her seat at the front, she introduced herself and allowed the teens to do the same.

After all the teens went around and said their names and ages, the teacher then enquired about whether they had all maintained a family tree and, if so, how many generations they had available. The twins and Mando had been keeping a family tree app on their personal computers since age ten. Mando's family tree went back ten generations, and he projected it on the wall for all to see. Then Nina shared her family tree, which traced back to the ancient Samurai more than two thousand years ago. The twins beamed with pride as they gauged how thoroughly impressed everyone was with their background.

Nina smiled sardonically as she took a seat and asked Celine to follow her up. Celine nervously explained to the class that she didn't have a family tree, and that this was her first time seeing one. Nina seemed quite satisfied.

As the instructor reassured Celine that it was fine that she didn't have one, Nina murmured to her sister, "I told you. Just an outback Martian nobody."

Anna shushed Nina to avoid drawing any attention from the instructor, but Celine heard the statement loud and clear. She lowered her head in embarrassment as blood flushed her cheeks.

Later that evening, Celine decided she would ask her father about their family tree. She desperately hoped that her Grandma

Enisi had given her dad one at some point, but his work had kept him too busy to share it.

Unfortunately, her hopes were in vain.

"That just wasn't something our ancestors did. But you can learn about our people by reading The History of the Cherokee Nation," he said.

"That's not a family tree, though," she responded despondently.

Her father sat in pensive silence for a moment. Finally, he proposed, "Why don't you make one? When you're on Earth, you can talk with the elders of our family, and they can give you names and dates."

Celine perked up. "That's a wonderful idea! Thanks, Dad. Tell Hannah I said hello, and please don't forget to Com me the second the baby arrives!"

The next day in class, Celine proudly shared the family tree that she had started. It contained her dad, mom, stepmom, her dad's brother, and her Grandma Enisi. The teacher praised her for her initiative, but Nina quickly interjected and explained that stepparents don't go on family trees.

"It's perfectly okay to have her stepmom on the tree," the instructor corrected. "Celine has a blended family."

That day, Celine left the class in a rather cheery mood, but when she passed Mr. Abiola on his way out of the Commons she immediately felt suspicious. He never socialized with the other passengers and often mumbled to himself.

"Are you enjoying the ship?" he asked as he strolled past her.

"Yes. Thank you for…" Celine stopped mid-sentence.

The blue shadow eerily trailed him.

CHAPTER 5

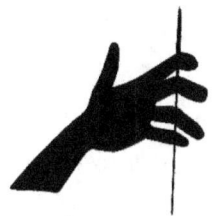

EXTRATERRESTRIALS

C eline ran nearly a kilometer to the administrative complex, passing the gym, the media room, and other rooms she didn't know existed, but not a single person in the hall. Any other time, she would have seen at least one guest. She was afraid to look back, afraid she might see the blue shadow trailing her.

At last, she reached the entrance to the complex. She paused to look around. *No blue shadow. Why is it taking so long to open this door?* Then the door slid open, and she stumbled into the room.

"I need to speak with the captain," Celine said to the lady sitting at the tall desk between her and the door labeled 'Captain'.

The stern-faced lady peered over the desk, staring down at the wide-eyed girl.

"There's an alien on this ship!" Celine exclaimed.

"I assure you that everyone on this ship belongs on this ship," she said as she crossed her arms as if to say you are not seeing anyone in here.

"But I saw a blue…"

Celine didn't know how to explain to someone who was unable to see auras.

"Young lady, if you're seeing unusual things, you need to visit the doctor, not the captain. You might be suffering from space sickness."

"So, I can't see the captain?" Celine said in anguish.

"Afraid not." The lady gave Celine a pitiful stare. "Do you need your bot to show you where the infirmary is?"

"No, ma'am. I know where it is."

Celine wanted to run past the lady and rush into the captain's office but decided to go to the infirmary instead. In the infirmary, Celine was told that all her vitals were normal, but she needed to drink more water.

"You realize that your body is made of 70% water, like planet Earth?"

"Yes, ma'am. I learned that in my science lessons."

"So, you know how important it is to stay hydrated."

"Yes, ma'am." Celine shook her head in a demure manner as she remembered passing the water station in the commons but not stopping to get any.

Then the doctor handed Celine a 2-liter bottle of water. "Drink one of these every day. This is your first time in deep space."

"Yes," said Celine as she licked her dry lips.

"You've only been here for an Earth week. Space sickness is normal for the first few weeks. If you're feeling discombobulated, hearing ringing in your ears or even hallucinating, let me know. We have medicine for that."

The doctor paused as in deep thought. Celine noticed a worried look on her face.

"The ship's artificial gravity has more force than what you're used to on Mars. It will get stronger as we get closer to Earth."

"I know. Dr. Baylor told me. She gave me some exercises for that."

"Good. Make sure you're in the gym every day. Do what you need to do to keep yourself healthy."

"I will."

Celine put the heavy water bottle under her arm and stepped into the hall. Floating next to the door was her Valet Bot, waiting for her. Boy, was she glad to see it!

"Take this back to my Pod," she said after taking several sips. She had to admit that the doctor was correct about her not drinking much water.

Maybe dehydration is causing me to hallucinate or *maybe I'm suffering from space sickness. I don't think so.*

However, recently she had seen a movie about extraterrestrials using mind control to get ordinary people to help them take over a spaceship. She wished she had not seen that movie, at least not during her spaceship trip.

But Mr. Abiola acts like he might be seeing what I'm seeing. What else could explain his suspicious behavior?

She had heard that Mr. Abiola was a bodyguard for a celebrity, but she never saw him with one, not even with the Ballingers. She was determined to figure out what he knew. She'd have to snoop around and ask seemingly innocent questions. She honored the Privacy Code, one of the most revered laws on Mars. But strange things were happening on the ship, right under everyone's noses, and it appeared only she and Mr. Abiola had noticed.

The next day, Celine awakened to Mando standing next to her Pod. She jerked away from him, about to kick the glass where he stood.

"Oh, I didn't mean to frighten you. I was checking to see if you were awake. You must have been very tired to have slept so late."

"What time is it? Aren't we using Earth's military time?"

"Yep! You've missed breakfast."

"You should have awakened me. Breakfast is my favorite meal."

"Sorry. I thought you needed the sleep."

Celine could see a concerned look on his face.

"I guess you forgot to tell your Bot to give you a new wake-up call," he said.

"Yes, I did." Celine bit her lower lip. "I'm sorry, Mando. It's not your fault that I missed breakfast. Everything is so different here. In the Compound, Ugi would wake me."

"Let me help you program your wake-up call. Put in your privacy code, so I can make the changes."

Celine did as he asked. "I want music," she said.

Mando smiled. "I know that," he mumbled and continued eyeing the small screen on the white wall beneath Celine's entry pad.

She watched Mando press a few buttons then the most delectable sounds of a flute permeated throughout her Pod and the lights softly brightened until they were bright as a Martian day. The sounds of a flute were her favorite music. She wondered how Mando knew that. She started to say *you're amazing* but simply said *thanks*. She liked Mando as a brother and besides, only Alex was amazing.

"I saw an Engineer Repair room in the bow of the ship. I think it would be an interesting place to do an interview."

"An interview?" Celine widened her eyes.

"I think your friend Alex would love a show about your adventures on the Fantasy."

"You think so?" Celine's smiled. She liked the idea of making Alex happy. "I noticed it too when I was doing my daily weight walk," she said, referring to the weighted vest she wore an hour a day to help maintain her newly found strength.

"Why not. Besides, it'll make the time on the ship go faster."

"What?" Celine twisted her lips to the right and stared at Mando. She wished Earthlings would say what they me.

"Forget it. Why don't you get something to eat and meet me at the Engineer Repair room at 1300 hours."

"Will do," said Celine. She was relieved that Mando didn't bother to explain *time flying*.

Learning so many Earthling sayings was tiring.

Heading to the Common, she was deterred by the vegetable garden. Unexpected fragrances drew her in. Like the flower garden on the other side of the ship, the vegetable garden was also a vertical garden. However, instead of flowers and spices growing up the sides of a burlap wall, there were vegetables, and Celine loved vegetables. There were never enough fresh vegetables on Mars.

She noticed the Smiths sitting quietly in the garden.

"Come join us, Celine," said Mrs. Smith.

Mr. Smith's surprised expression over his wife's invitation did not go unnoticed by Celine. The couple seemed to like Celine, but she felt uncomfortable around them because they were always kissing each other on the mouth and touching each other in all the wrong places. Celine was not used to seeing affection shown so openly in public.

I guess that's what newlyweds do on Earth.

"No thanks," she said nervously. "I am going to grab a salad to go."

"Wonder why young folks are always in a hurry," he said to his wife who smiled.

"And where is your Valet Bot?" he asked.

"Waiting at my Pod. I hope," she said as she began to pile a to-go bamboo box with every vegetable from the buffet.

"It's always a good idea to have your Bot around," he said. "You'll never know when you might need it."

His Bot sat in the corner in resting mode.

"Hey, sleepy head," Mr. Smith said to the Bot.

The Bot lit up and whistled.

"Bring me some of that mint tea and bring my lovely bride some tomato juice."

It floated over to the meal station that sat in the center of the room, only a few feet from the Smiths. In a matter of minutes, it was floating next to Mr. Smith with a glass of iced mint tea held in one pincer and freshly made tomato juice in the other.

"See what I mean?" he said before taking a sip of tea and then smacking his lips with pleasure.

"Yes, sir," she said.

"Did you hear that, honey?" he said to his bride. "What a fine young lady. Great manners."

Mr. Smith had an assertive personality. Celine felt if he believed in extraterrestrials, he could influence the other guests. Seeing he was in such a good mood, she decided to ask him his thoughts about extraterrestrials.

"Mr. Smith, may I ask you a question?" she said.

"Sure, honey." He stretched out the word honey as if he was singing.

"Do you believe in extraterrestrials?"

As soon as she saw the expression on his face, she knew it was the wrong thing to do.

"What?" He turned to his wife. "What's this gal talking about?"

Mrs. Smith gulped down her freshly made juice, then burst into laughter.

"She wants to know if you believe in ETs," she said as she watched her husband's confused expression. "You know, little green men!"

"No, we don't!" Mrs. Smith said and continued to laugh.

"Why on earth would you ask me something like that?" Mr. Smith asked Celine,

who was beginning to wonder the same thing.

On Mars, all the colonists believed there was intelligent life on other planets.

"It's just something I was thinking about, sir," she muttered as she backed her way toward the entrance, where she stopped and plucked a tempting ripe red tomato from a vine, then stepped into the hall where she devoured it and the rest of her salad.

No nibbling.

"Such nonsense!" was the last thing she heard Mr. Smith say about her.

How will I ever convince the captain there's an alien on this ship if the captain can't see it, and no one takes me seriously?

She continued her route to the Engineering repair room when she noticed a man who was wearing a red jacket labeled Engineering Repair, Ray Lambert.

"We might be heading to the same place," she said cheerfully.

He looked down at his label. "Yes, if you're heading to Repairs."

"I'm meeting a friend. We're recording our stay on the Fantasy."

"Is your Bot helping you?"

Celine looked over her shoulder into the metal face of her floating Bot.

"You again," she said with frustration.

"It's doing its job," said the engineer.

"I guess so. It's just—I'm not used to being followed. It doesn't give me much space."

The engineer chuckled. "I've done some work on Mars and, as I recalled, no one had much space there."

Celine chuckled. "You're right."

As they continued down the hall, she noticed Mando waiting next to the Repair room. He had his large recording camera hanging across his shoulder.

"Oh, there's my friend."

Celine waved to get Mando's attention. "Mando!"

Mando's face lit up when he saw her.

"I can't get the door to open," he said.

"Let me help you with the door," said the engineer. "Give me a moment and I'll get us in."

The engineer pushed RAY. The reader beeped and the door slid open.

"After you," he said to the teens.

Before stepping into the room, Celine turned to her Bot.

"Not you," she said.

The Bot made a quick stop and veered to the right of the door, floated to the floor, then went into rest mode.

"Oh my," said Celine. "I can't get rid of it."

Stepping into the room, she expected to see several engineers repairing broken Bots. But was surprised to see a pasty-looking thin man with a head of dark hair sitting alone at a desk, monitoring a three-dimensional map of the outside of the ship.

The engineer stepped next to him.

"Mr. Doolittle, I've brought you some of our guests. They're making a recording of their experiences on the Fantasy."

Mr. Doolittle seemed to perk up for a moment.

"You have your work assignment?" he asked the engineer, who nodded and went into another room.

"Mr. Dolittle, I hope you don't mind us recording you," Celine said.

"That's not my name," said the man. "The name's D'Entremont-Latour."

"Oh, sorry. But .."

"Not your fault. It's his way of joking."

"Mr. D'Entra.. ahh sorry."

"Call me Mr. D."

"Wonderful, Mr. D'Entremont-Latour," said Mando. "May we record you?"

Celine opened her eyes in amazement. "I didn't know you spoke French."

Mando's grin spread from ear to ear.

"Sure. Record, but don't touch," said Mr. D. "There's nothing much happening in here though." He looked toward the glass room where the engineer was gathering tools.

"Is he going out into Space?" asked Celine.

"Yes. That's his job to make repairs to the ship."

Celine detected a bit of envy in his voice.

Mando turned so his camera faced the engineer and Celine moved in closer.

The engineer went into a small adjoining decontamination room where he appeared to be inhaling from an oxygen tank.

"Why is he doing that?" Mando asked.

"He's getting ready to go outside to make some repairs and he's pre-breathing pure oxygen, so he doesn't get the Bends. You know what that is, don't you?" Then Mr. D went on to answer his own question. "It's a decompression sickness."

"I know what the Bends is," Celine said.

She continued to watch the engineer through the glass wall. She watched him step into a white hugely padded radiation suit that automatically shut behind him. Then he checked his suit's equipment. She watched him check his pure oxygen level at 100% and air pressure normal, and then he pushed a button on his sleeve that Celine was not familiar with. He put on his helmet which fastened automatically, and then pushed the number 224 on the code pad and opened the airlock. She watched him plug in a tether from the ship to his suit and then he stepped into space onto a metal bridge that appeared to wrap around the ship. The heavy door closed behind him. The teens watched him hold the rails as he inched forward. A Bot joined him, and they moved further around the disk-shaped part of the ship until they were out of sight.

"Wow!"

"Looks exciting, doesn't it?" said the thin man. His weary eyes showed a bit of envy.

"Yes, but that suit looks hot, and I didn't see a fan in it. How does the engineer keep cool?" Celine asked. She had seen similar suits at the Compound, but they all had fans in them.

"The suit's full of water."

"Water? But how?"

"It's a water-cooled garment. Did you see him push that button on the right sleeve? It seals the water in the suit and keeps it away from the helmet."

"Oh. What happens if the water gets in the helmet?"

"Nothing, if he's in this ship. But outside in zero gravity, the water would rise into the helmet, possibly drowning him."

Celine shuddered, then returned her attention to the map.

"What's this?" she said as Mando swerved the camera toward the map.

"I use this map to check the ship for damages," Mr. D. said and rolled his eyes toward the ceiling. "I get to watch the engineers and Bots have all the fun. My job is to stare at this map and let the engineers know when something needs to be done. We had a mild solar storm last night, and it damaged two of the solar panels. That's what Eric is repairing now."

"Your job is important too," Celine said. "I'm so glad you found the damaged solar panels."

The man started to say something but simply stared at Celine.

"I'm from the Martian colony."

"I figured that," he said with embarrassment. "You Martians seem to find pleasure in work."

"Yes, we do, but I'm learning to enjoy the fun and freedom we have on the Fantasy."

The man nodded. "Well, do you have any more questions?"

"Yes, I do," said Celine. She paused for a moment trying to decide whether she should ask her question. *I have to ask it.*

"If an alien, I mean an ET was on the Fantasy, where could it take control of this ship?"

Mando took the camera down from his shoulder and turned it off.

"Certainly not from here," he said, then brayed with laughter.

"Thank you for that joke," he said as he held his chest. "Sometimes I need a bit of humor.

And being the polite person Celine was taught to be, she said, "You're welcome."

As soon as she and Mando stepped into the hall, he shook his head no as he stared at Celine.

"Why did you ask that?" he said.

"I had to. I can't explain it yet, but there is something supernatural happening on this ship."

As the ship moved further from Mars, it began to pick up speed. The ship's maximum speed, powered by nuclear fusion, would be 175,000 kilometers per hour, fast but nowhere near the speed of light.

Even so, becoming accustomed to the speed became a problem for several of the guests, especially Celine. By the third day, the speed had given her a headache and she felt a little queasy after each meal, and even the foods that tasted great when the ship was near Mars began to taste different—not bad, but not as delicious. These were her complaints in the infirmary, along with Mr. Monroe, one of the Mars investors.

"This is your first trip in deep space," the doctor said to both of her patients. "This is all normal for deep space travel. You'll feel more like yourself in a few days."

So, for three days, Celine spent most of her time in her Pod. She was too sick to follow a blue shadow if she had seen it and too sick to investigate Mr. Abiola. She only focused on feeling well. Her Valet Bot came in handy, bringing her soups, juices, and water to keep her hydrated.

Just as she was feeling better, Dr. Vee came by to see her. Of the four teens, she was his favorite. He had said she reminded him of himself—like a fish out of water.

"How are you feeling?"

"Better than yester - SOL," she replied.

"Yesterday, not SOL. We're on Earth's time," Dr. Vee corrected her.

"We will be having a teen's meeting on Monday," he continued. "You think you can make it?"

"I'll try. Oops." Celine quickly put her hand over her mouth as if making certain not to say any more along those lines. She remembered the word 'try' was rarely used on Mars. The word was associated with failure, and on Mars failure was not an option.

"I will be there," she corrected herself.

Two days later, on Monday, Celine was feeling like her normal self and was the first person in the Media room. Dr. Vee followed shortly. He seemed very impressed that she was there before him. He called her punctual and a real role model.

Finally, the other teens arrived, and Celine noticed a crossed-eyed look Nina gave Anna after the two girls saw her.

Must be that lazy left eye. It looks real but it has no aura in front of it.

After everyone had taken a seat, Dr. Vee began his lesson about safety procedures and asked questions that came from the safety manual. It was obvious that Celine knew the materials and Dr. Vee mentioned that several times.

"Teacher's pet," whispered Nina, loud enough for Celine to hear but not loud enough to get herself in trouble.

One of the most important rules of the ship was to respect each other's privacy.

"Why?" asked Anna, who seemed concerned.

"Our guests demand it. They are very private people."

"What happens if the privacy code is broken?

"You will get in some serious trouble."

Dr. Vee stomped his foot.

"Please! Read the manual," he said. Then as if speaking another language, he exclaimed, "Zit, zat, zat!"

His face turned a bright red and then his stomach made a loud grumble which made everyone laugh, including Dr. Vee, in embarrassment. Then he was his usual smiling self.

"This meeting is over," he said.

Everyone but Celine gave a sigh of relief.

"Let's head back to the garden," said Nina.

"Sister, I don't think we..." Anna said, but Nina ignored her and headed for the door.

"Come on, sister. I'm sure there's a good movie playing soon."

Celine noticed that Anna reluctantly joined her sister.

Before the girls could leave, Dr. Vee reminded everyone to return to class after lunch for the science lecture about the wonderful world of insects.

"Oh, yuck!" said all the teens.

"I hate creepy crawlies," said Nina. "I thought when we left the Compound we had gotten away from those critters," Nina said and smiled at Celine.

Celine quickly looked away. Just once, Nina had seen a roach in the cargo area. It had survived its trip in space, only to be flattened by a cargo man. It was one of the first experiences the twins had in the Compound and they wouldn't let Celine forget it, even though they knew it embarrassed her.

"Will they ever be my friends?" asked Celine of Mando.

"Don't worry about it," said Mando.

"That's no answer," Celine said in exasperation.

"You take things too seriously. That's why they're always joking with you."

Maybe I'm trying too hard. I thought I was just being myself.

Celine decided to grab a salad from the vegetable garden and go back to her Pod to have lunch alone. She looked at her cute Robo Pug lying on her bed. She wanted to turn it on and play with it, but thought should finish her meal to avoid a sad-eyed stare and pleading for food it couldn't eat. When she had finished her meal, she picked up her pug and turned it on. It seemed happy to see her. It wagged its tail and licked her chin.

"You're my friend," she said. "You never tease me. You're always happy to see me."

Suddenly, her pug began to growl. She opened her Pod and saw the blue shadow heading down the hall toward the community bathroom. Her pug jumped off the bed and ran after it.

It's real. Puggie sees it.

"Come back, Puggie!" she called as she ran after it.

The shadow, with Puggie on its heels, rounded the corner of the hall and she couldn't see either.

By the time she reached the end of the hall, the barking had stopped. She knew why when she turned the corner and saw Puggie lying on its back with its short legs sticking straight up, not moving at all. There was a strange golden jewel attached to Puggie's forehead.

CHAPTER 6

ARGUMENTS

"This is a fashion taser," The doctor told Celine as she removed it from Puggie's forehead. "Some of the wealthy teens wear these on their clothing. They're dangerous weapons as far as I'm concerned. If your pug had been a live dog, he would have been temporarily paralyzed. Where did this thing come from?"

Celine didn't hear anything the doctor said. She just wanted Puggie repaired.

"Doctor, can you fix him? Please?"

"He's not broken," the doctor said. "Just zapped and battery-drained."

"So, get him an energy pack or plug him into an electric outlet?" Celine asked.

"Yep! Plug in the pug and he'll be good as new," laughed the doctor. "Have you seen anyone wearing this taser? Do you have any idea who could have done this?"

"No, ma'am. Not yet, but I'm working on it."

The next day in class, the media teacher's lesson was about debating skills. Ms. Lex said debating skills are the most important part of a teenager's curriculum because it teaches students how to speak and defend their ideas.

She asked them to pick a topic, and since no one spoke up Celine did. She hoped this would be a way to get everyone talking about extraterrestrials.

"Why don't we have a debate about the possibility of extraterrestrials," she said.

"Interesting topic," said Ms. Lex. "Any reason why you picked that particular topic?"

"I think we might need to know about this."

"Okay. Are there any other topics?" the instructor asked.

None of the other teens said anything until Mando spoke up.

"Good topic, Celine." He gave her a thumbs-up and a wink.

"Okay. Then that will be our topic," said Ms. Lex.

She sat at her desk, spoke commands to her computer, and pulled up an image of a large graphic organizer.

"When debating a topic, you need to consider the pros and the cons."

She paused for the teens to pull up the same image on their computers and to record and write their notes.

She continued, "The pros are the supporting evidence that extraterrestrials exist."

She paused. "The cons are the supporting evidence that extraterrestrials do not exist."

She waited then asked, "Are there any questions?"

No one had questions, so she continued.

"Which of you believes that there are extraterrestrials?"

Celine was the only one who raised her hand.

"So, Celine, you will find evidence to support the idea. Mando, you will be her partner.

"Nina and Anna, you two will work together."

The teacher said she would give the teens two hours to do their research and they could take a break every twenty minutes if they wanted. Then she left the media room. As soon as the door closed behind her, Nina began to taunt Celine.

"So, the Martian girl believes in little green men?" laughed Nina.

Anna covered her mouth, but it was obvious that she found the joke funny.

"Let's work in the Commons," said Mando.

"Great idea," said Celine and they left a wide-eyed Nina watching them as they left.

When Celine and Mando returned to the media room an hour later, their assignment was completed. The twins were still working. Since Ms. Lex had not returned and Celine and Mando had completed their research, they decided to study for their next science test.

When Ms. Lex returned exactly two hours later, the twins were just finishing the research. The instructor was happy to see that her students could work and complete their tasks independently.

"Now, I'm giving you the rules for your debate," she said, "and I want you to decide which person will speak for your team. Okay?"

Mando said he wanted Celine to speak since she was the one who believed in their topic, and Ms. Lex agreed. She turned to the twins.

"Who's speaking for your team?" she asked and was surprised that Anna who normally followed her sister's lead said she would. Anna justified that she should because she had done most of the research and felt like she should be the one to present it.

"Okay. Here are your debate rules."

Suddenly, a list of rules flashed onto the wall.

Debate Rules:

Content : What you will actually say in the debate.

Argument (whole): The case your team is making must be outlined in the introduction. State your main arguments and state the general thrust of your case.

Argument (part): Put your best argument first. Justify your arguments with basic logic, examples, and quotes.

Nina laughed when she saw the notes.

"You should do well on this assignment, Anna. You argue all the time."

"This is not that kind of argument," said Ms. Lex. "It's more like a timed oral presentation with rebuttals."

"Oh, I get it," said Celine.

Nina hissed. Celine gave a side glance in her direction.

"Let's get back to the notes," said Ms. Lex. "Are there any questions before we go to the next page?"

"No," the teens said in unison since it was getting close to lunchtime, and the enticing scents of the chef-prepared meals were seeping into the classroom

Rebuttal (parts): Arguments can be factually, morally, or logically flawed. They may be misinterpreted. Example: state the other team's argument and explain why it is flawed.

Rebuttal (whole): Systematically break down the other team's arguments, especially their most important ones.

"Gosh!" complained Nina. "Do we have to type all of that?"

"Young lady!" said Ms. Lex as she folded her arms across her chest.

"Okay, I'm doing it. Can we just read it and record it?"

"Yes, after you have typed it into your notes."

"Why?" Nina whined, and slid down in her chair.

"I want you to think of your brain as a file manager," Ms. Lex said matter-of-factly.

Anna snickered. Nina rolled her eyes in Anna's direction.

Ms. Lex continued, "When you write something, it goes into one file. Then when you say something, it goes into another file."

"Wow! I didn't know that," said Mando.

Ms. Lex continued, "It's better to have the information in two files instead of one. Don't you agree?"

"Yes," said Nina musingly. However, she still had a sour face toward her sister.

"Now get busy," demanded the teacher.

"I'm finished," said Celine. "May I go into the hall so I can read it aloud?"

The teacher nodded. "When you are finished," she told the students, "you are dismissed. Presentations will be in the Commons tomorrow before all the ship's guests. A few of the crew will also be there. They will vote and decide the winning team."

Then Ms. Lex left the room, which meant her instruction had ended.

Celine was so excited that she would have the opportunity to get everyone on the ship thinking about extraterrestrials. This brought a smile to her face because only a few days ago no one she spoke to about ETs wanted to talk about it. Now she would have everyone talking about ETs and maybe warning them in the process.

Puggie was sitting up on the bed when Celine returned to her Pod. He wagged his tail and barked when he saw her. Celine picked him up and hugged him.

"Oh, Puggie! You're well!" She looked at his forehead. There was no residual damage.

Puggie licked her face.

"That blue shadow is real. I didn't imagine it. I wasn't hallucinating. You saw it, too. Didn't you, boy?"

"Woof," her robotic dog said as if it agreed.

After playing with Puggie, Celine went to the Commons. It was strange to go there and find it empty. She sat in one of the fluffy white chairs to organize her ideas for the debate.

Later Venera came in and saw Celine sitting alone and decided to join her. For many reasons, the young girl reminded Venera of herself. As a teen, she was the outsider who always tried to fit in.

"Mind if I join you?" she asked as she sat in the plush chair next to Celine.

"I was just finishing my practice for tomorrow's debate," said the tired student.

"Oh. Yes, I heard about the debate. I'm looking forward to it."

Venera continued. "Celine, I've noticed a little friction between you and the other girls on the ship."

Celine sucked her teeth and twisted in her seat.

"Is it that obvious?"

She wrapped her arms around her chest.

"I don't understand why they're always putting me down."

"Often people mistreat others because they have issues with themselves."

"I hadn't thought of it that way," Celine said thoughtfully.

"When I was your age, other girls thought I was strange."

"But you were raised on Earth, weren't you? I thought they were making fun of me because I'm a Martian."

Venera flinched. Celine noticed it and wondered why.

"I was born on Mars and my friend Alex calls me Martian girl," Celine said to clarify her reason for calling herself a Martian.

Come to think of it, I haven't heard from Alex in quite a while. I wonder what he's doing. I haven't even told him that I'm coming to Earth. Won't he be surprised?

"That makes sense," Venera said in response to Celine's explanation.

"Yes, I was raised on Earth, but... Never mind. That's a long story."

"I don't mind long stories," Celine said. She was eager for a distraction from her schoolwork.

"My family believes that our ancestors didn't start out on Earth."

CHAPTER 7

WHERE IS THE ET?

Celine's eyes widened when Venera told her that her ancestors didn't come from Earth. She wondered if Venera was making this up to teach her a lesson. Sometimes, her Grandma Enisi would tell her stories to make a point. The curious teen continued to listen.

"All my life, I've been told that some alien race brought my ancestors to Earth."

"Oh!" Celine said in surprise, unconsciously leaning away from Venera.

Celine wanted to say, *What a strange story.* Instead, she continued to listen, hoping that a lesson would be taught.

"My planet was at war, and warring factions released several hydrogen bombs on the planet."

"Oh, that's an awful story," the adolescent said. She stared wide-eyed, wondering where this story would lead.

"Yes, it is. It affected the electromagnetic field around our planet. Do you know what that is?"

The schoolgirl thought for a moment. "It's a force that can protect a planet from radiation."

"Right. At first, the scientists didn't notice. But the planet began to lose its atmosphere, then finally groundwater."

Celine was letting all the story sink in as she waited to hear more.

Venera continued, "By that time, the people had begun to live underground, deep in the caves, some in the lava tubes."

"They had underground cities like the one we're building on Mars?"

"No, they were not prosperous like your Mars colony. They had no one to bring them supplies or equipment. They were on their own, barely surviving, when young couples started disappearing from the caves. One of the couples was my great-grandmother and great- grandfather one-thousand generations ago. They were brought to Earth. That's the story I was told by my mother."

"Wow, that's a cool story."

"Thanks, Celine. It's just a story. I have no proof. So, that's why some of the other kids made fun of me."

"Because of your family's story?"

"Yes. Because we believed our ancestral history was different."

"People from Earth are so difficult to understand. On Mars…" Celine searched for the right words.

"On Mars, the colonists are like one big family. We all try to get along."

Venera chuckled.

"Well, it's certainly not like that on Earth. I wish it was. Maybe one day it will be."

Then Venera was silent as if in deep thought. She inhaled deeply and her eyes lit up.

"I have an idea that I think will help you win over the twins."

"Really?" The news was too good to be true, but Celine was ready to try most anything Venera suggested.

"I overheard the twins say that they have a birthday coming up. Why don't you plan a surprise party for them?"

"A party? I don't know how to plan a party. We didn't have parties on Mars."

"I'll help you. We could do a tea party. This will be so much fun. On the Fantasy, we're always looking for a reason to have a party!"

"So I've noticed," Celine mumbled, because on Mars the colonists were the opposite; always looking for a job to be done or a problem to be solved. So many parties made her feel strangely out of place.

"The twins love parties! We'll have to give them what they like so they'll appreciate it."

"Okay. I'll do it! But I'll work on it after the debate."

"Of course, and I'll be rooting for your debate team."

"Thanks, Venera."

The next day, all the students arrive at the Commons early to get set up for the debate. Ms. Lex had the students sit at facing tables near her Podium. This made Celine feel like she was going to be in combat.

Then the unimaginable happened. Celine noticed Mr. Abiola and the blue shadow entering. Surprisingly, the shadow actually sat down on the couch next to him. She tensed her fists and began to stare angrily at the shadow.

"Are you okay?" asked Mando as he looked toward the couch, where he saw Mr. Abiola.

Celine nodded yes. Then Ms. Lex asked Celine and Anna if they were ready to present, and they were. They were told they would have three minutes to present their arguments and only two minutes for their rebuttals. Celine was to present first. When she turned back to stare down the shadow it was gone, but Mr. Abiola was still there. The nervous student walked shyly to the spot where Ms. Lex had asked them to stand when presenting and slowly began her presentation.

"Most scientists agree that aliens certainly exist in the universe. The Milky Way Galaxy contains millions of stars and these stars, like our sun, have planets traveling around them as Earth and Mars travel around our sun. Our galaxy, The Milky Way, is just one of the 200 billion galaxies in the known universe. It's all in the numbers that extraterrestrials have a high probability to exist."

After hearing the applause, she walked confidently back to her chair. Then Anna walked quickly before the audience to present her arguments. She put her right hand on her hip and began.

"How many of you have seen an alien?" Anna seemed pleased that no one responded. "Where are they?" Anna paused to let her argument sink in. Celine thought Anna was doing a great job connecting with the audience. Anna continued.

"I'm sure you are aware of the Fermi Paradox. According to Fermi, this universe is about 4.5 billion years old. So, with basic technology, aliens could have colonized the entire universe by now. With the technology we have, we can colonize every habitable planet, moon, or asteroid in our galaxy within five hundred years. In fact, we have astronauts who will be landing on Europa, one of Jupiter's seventy-five moons very soon. If there's intelligent life out there and at least as intelligent as us, where are they? Why haven't we seen them?"

The audience gave Anna equally loud applause. She smiled at Celine with a closed mouth and pranced to her chair next to her sister.

Celine stood from her chair and began the rebuttal to Anna's arguments.

"There might be civilizations in the universe whose technology is as good as ours, and for some reason they don't want us to see them, or there are aliens involved in wars or some other kinds of problems on their planet. Maybe they are beings that we cannot see with the average vision." Celine awkwardly placed her right hand on her hip and asked,

"Did you know that the average human can only see less than one percent of the light spectrum? We cannot assume that extraterrestrials can be seen with normal vision or even want to be seen by us. I still say the numbers favor the possibility of intelligent life on other planets. There are billions of planets in the known universe, and I am certain that some of them have life on them."

The audience applauded loudly for her.

"You did a good job," Mando said to the exhausted, but proud, girl as she sat down next to him.

Anna presented her rebuttal and received just as much applause as Celine did.

"You stomped her like an insect," Nina said to her sister as she sat next to her.

Ms. Lex said she was very impressed with both teams' presenters. But she would now ask the guests to vote for the winning team on the keypads on the arm of their seats. When Ms. Lex computed the votes, she realized that there was a tie. She stepped into the hall and motioned for Dr. Vee to join her in the hall for a recount. She told Dr. Vee her dilemma, who said that was easy to solve. Since he had not voted, he would vote for Celine.

"That settles it," the teacher said.

They both reentered the Commons. Dr. Vee returned to his seat next to Mr. Abiola and gave him an all-knowing wink. Ms. Lex went to the front of the audience and called the teams to stand next to her. She praised the teams and said both teams would receive a letter grade of E for excellence. Then she removed the four Debate Pins from the table. They looked like a golden star with the word Debate engraved on them.

"All of my students are winners, don't you agree?"

Everyone applauded and nodded with smiling faces.

"However, the winners of today's debate are Celine and Mando!"

"Yes!" yelled Celine in an uncharacteristic manner and then Mando gave her a fist bump.

Everyone applauded, including the twins, but once the students returned to their seats, Nina told her sister, "Next debate, we will pick the topic."

Celine hoped that her presentation got the guests thinking. She knew she would find out what the blue shadow was, and she didn't want people to be so surprised. She might have to figure out a way to capture it without being hurt. But strangely, she didn't see the blue shadow anymore after her debate. She also noticed that Mr. Abiola wasn't in the Commons for meals anymore but was having his meals in his suite.

CHAPTER 8

WHAT A PARTY!

The next day, Celine and Venera met in the Media room. Together they did research on how to plan a Japanese party. They hoped to plan the best birthday party for Anna and Nina, who were of Japanese descent. They found out that a good Japanese party should have a flower ceremony and a tea ceremony. They decided to make dozens of chrysanthemums, the most revered flower in Japan. Celine would code the 3-D printer and load it with red and white synthetics to make the flowers. They would ask the chef to fix Japanese dishes like sushi, Miso soup, and Chicken Teriyaki.

"And rice pudding for dessert," said Celine.

"I don't think rice pudding is a Japanese dish," said Venera.

"Oh, I love rice pudding. I tried it yesterday. We should have some."

Venera shook her head no and gave the wide-eyed girl a motherly smile.

"I'll ask the chef if he can get red azuki beans for Wagashi for dessert."

"What's that?" The teen wiggled her nose as she mumbled *Wagashi*.

"It's like a pasty cookie that would go great with the tea served at the tea ceremony."

"Pasty? Oh yummy," Celine said unconvincingly.

"You'll love it. Now let's get back to planning this party. We'll need to program the printer for pink origami to hang on the walls, and we'll have paper lanterns and fans. Everyone will wear a kimono; I'll make them. And we'll have the band play music for an original Kabuki dance. Everything will be perfect!" Venera said all in one breath.

Celine was beginning to feel excited about the party.

"This will be the best party ever!" she said.

Meanwhile, the twins were sitting on their bed together in their Pod. No one was in the sleeping hall but them.

"I wonder if Dr. Vee will tell everyone about our birthday," said Anna longingly.

"Why should he?" said Nina.

Anna looked at her younger sister, who was younger by a few minutes. She wondered when she would change. Most of the time she was either angry or sad.

"I think he's a nice man and he wants us to be happy. So why not?"

That was just the right amount of confrontation, though it didn't take much to anger Nina.

"That's your problem. You think everyone is nice!" She looked at Anna with disdain.

Anna was not in the mood to be bullied or put down by her sister. Her sister had a habit of sucking the joy out of a simple conversation.

"What's wrong with looking for the good in people?" she said. "You should try it sometime."

Nina's well-practiced response rolled off her tongue like a laser cutting through plastic.

"How can you say that when you're not good?"

"Nina, let's not go there again. Please."

Anna wondered what it would take for her sister to stop blaming her for something she had no control over.

"Well, you're not the little good twin everyone thinks you are."

Nina's words continued their assault.

"When we were joined in our mother's womb, you tried to kill me."

"Stop it!" Anna cried. "How can a fetus know?"

"It's who you are, and I will never let you forget what you took from me!"

"I will not listen to this," Anna wailed as she jumped down from the bunk and ran out of the sleeping hall.

"Come back here!" Nina screamed. "You'll be sorry. You think I didn't notice your snicker when Ms. Lex was talking about the brain?"

Anna stopped for a moment. "I was not laughing at you!"

"You were! But you won't be laughing when we have the science test because this Brain Computer Implant will find the test key, and guess who's not sharing!"

Anna and Nina both hated science and never studied for their tests. Nina would always use her Brain Computer Implant (BCI) to infiltrate the teacher's answer key and share it on her sister's computer test pad.

"I won't be helping you cheat on the test tomorrow," Nina mumbled. "I'll get the 'E' and maybe you'll get a common 'C'. I don't care."

Celine and Venera had done a lot of research to make the twins' birthday party a success. They had learned that the kimono—a silk robe—symbolized longevity and good fortune. They were happy that everyone had agreed to wear one. Venera printed polyester kimonos, which she said would look like real silk. She made the robes with long sleeves that flowed from the shoulder to the floor for the females and shorter sleeves for the males. Their Valet Bots also helped, making paper lanterns with automatic candles and placing one on each table beside a single red rose. Mando had told Celine, just in time, before she made the chrysanthemums, that they were not appropriate.

"Chrysanthemums are very popular in Japan," he said, "but they're usually seen at funerals, not birthday parties."

So, she made deep red roses instead. The single red rose next to the white lantern created the delicate simplicity she had hoped for.

"Careful," Venera yelled at her bot who quickly floated back and forth near the high ceilings, hanging red paper dragons that looked like bouncing springs with a big friendly head on one end and a fish tail fin on the other. The Commons was beginning to take on the party atmosphere.

All the guests were to bring a present, a Haiku poem, or a talent to present to the twins before the tea ceremony. Green tea was to be served from delicately made cups that looked like fine china. The pastries would be served with the tea. All the foods were being prepared by the chefs and would be brought to the Commons at the appropriate time. The chefs even prepared a dish of rice pudding just for Celine. Finally, everything was ready. Both Venera and Celine were exhausted, but when they stood in the Commons admiring the elegantly decorated room and checking everything on their list, they agreed it had been fun and they couldn't wait to see everyone enjoying their handiwork.

"Maybe we should have more parties on Mars," Celine told Venera, who smiled.

"Maybe they should, but they do what they must do. I'm sure."

Celine.

As Celine dressed for the party, remembering to put the left side of the robe over the right so as to not offend and to tie her sash up high above her waist, she felt a little nervous. She had decided to play her flute as a gift to the twins. This would be the first time she had played it outside of family and friends at the Compound. She knew the twins, especially Nina, were critical of her. Her hands shook as she removed the bagged flute from her drawer below her bed.

I should have written a poem. That would be a lot easier.

Venera and Celine arrived early. They wanted to check on the food and to put any final touches on the decorations. Celine was wearing a shiny red kimono with bronzy threads that appeared like flowers and her gray boots.

"You look lovely," said Venera.

"Thanks, and so do you."

Celine's grandmother had taught her to never accept a compliment without giving one, and so she did. Thinking of her grandmother gave her an achy feeling in her chest. She had not heard anything about her grandmother since coming on the Fantasy. She had to assume that no news was good news.

"Did you make a gift?" asked Venera as she noticed the cloth bag that Celine held tightly in her right hand.

"I'm going to play my flute," the girl said as confidently as she could muster.

"Wonderful. I can't wait to hear it."

"Thanks."

Then the guests began to enter the ballroom. The Smiths came in dressed in almost identical red and white kimonos. They looked fabulous; however, Mr. Smith, who was very tall, seemed a little awkward in his kimono since the hem stopped at his knees instead of his ankles.

"Only for you," he told Venera, who chuckled.

Even Mr. Abiola came into the ballroom, wearing a turquoise kimono that matched his left eye. He smiled with his lips closed. Something about that seemed insincere to Celine. She found herself mimicking his closed-lip smile back at him as she tried to figure out why the blue shadow was usually near him.

Finally, all the guests had arrived and were mingling about as they waited for Dr. Vee to bring the twins to the ballroom.

The girls knew the party was for them and everyone expected them to wear something exquisite. The twins did not disappoint. They entered the ballroom wearing red and gold kimonos with wide gold-colored sashes. They wore identical headdresses made of red silk-like flowers. Golden butterflies with ruby red abdomens dangled from golden sticks that pierced the red flowers in their upswept hair.

Celine wondered how they could have created something so uniquely beautiful. They had to have done each other's headpieces. *It must be nice to have a twin sister.*

The twins glided to the special table reserved for them. Everyone took a seat and the Bots brought out the sweets. Celine remembered to take only one and to nibble. She would do all things right and the twins would know she could be a worthy friend. After the sweets, the Bots brought out Koicha green tea, which she drank despite not liking the flavor.

Finally, Venera called the guests up to present their gifts. When called, Celine swallowed and went to the center of the room to sit in a chair in front of the twin's table. Nina arched her eyebrows when Celine said she would play on her flute a song that had been passed down for generations through her father's family. Her dad had taught it to her. It was a song she would play for the twins and in honor of her grandmother.

"I hope you will love it as much as I do."

Celine opened the cloth bag and pulled out her wrapped instrument. She unwrapped it with reverence, a plainly carved wooden flute, lightweight but as long as her lower arm. When she held it up, some guests gasped!

"It's made of wood. No one makes anything out of wood anymore," whispered Mrs. Ballenger.

"It must be very old. It's so beautiful!" said Mrs. Smith.

Celine licked her lips and, with nervous fingers, lifted the flute to her mouth and began to blow. The rich, hauntingly beautiful sounds began to fill the room. Everyone was mesmerized. Even the Valet Bots stopped serving. All things were silent except the music that flowed from Celine's flute. She played the song for her grandma. It was a healing song. She hoped her grandma somehow could hear it and was getting well. She remembered the times when she might think of her grandma and her Grandma Enisi would call her. "We're on the same wavelength," her grandma would say, and then chuckle. "We both have those good vibrations."

Listen, Grandmother. Hear the healing song.

When she finished playing, everyone was still silent.

"Oh, I feel wonderful," said Mrs. Ballenger.

Mando looked at Celine with adoration.

"I didn't know you could play the flute like that. That was incredible."

Then everyone applauded, even the twins.

I did it and the twins liked it.

Then Nina said, "Let's dance!" as she pulled Mando toward the dance floor.

Venera told the musicians to start the dance music. There were drummers and flutists.

"Ah. Real music at last," said Nina under her breath. "Mando, let's show everyone how to dance the Odori!"

Mando was grinning from ear to ear and loving all of the attention he was getting from such a beautiful girl.

He bowed with prayerful hands and a bent waist. Then Nina bowed. She raised her arms so the long sleeves of her kimono could hang down and flow as she moved her arms. Mando raised his arms and mirrored Nina's movements. Celine thought it was so beautifully elegant.

"Come everyone, let's join them in a circle," said Venera.

"Come next to me," Mando said to Celine.

No one noticed that flash of anger in Nina's left eye as she looked at Mando, who was smiling at Celine as she learned the dance. The drumbeats and flute in the band continued, and everyone was laughing and seemed to be enjoying themselves; except Nina, who seemed to be in deep thought.

Celine felt the party was a success. But at the end of the party, one of the guests started screaming.

"Leave me alone!" His hands cupped his ears. "Shut up! Stop it!"

"What's going on?" asked Mando, then quickly ran over to the loud man.

Dr. Vee called security immediately. "Get someone here quickly. It's Mr. Monroe again. Let the doc know. He's delirious! Oh no!" Dr. Vee screamed. "Don't let him get near the airlocks."

Mando, who was closest to Mr. Monroe, dove onto the man's legs and they both fell to the floor. The man looked deeply into Mando's eyes.

"They're out there. Don't you hear them?" he said.

Mando could see the terror in the man's eyes.

The medical doctor and his team ran into the Commons, surrounded the man and, with Mando's help, held him down on the floor. Then the doctor jabbed Mr. Monroe in the shoulder with a hypo, while Mando held his head still. Mr. Monroe, who had been kicking and trying his best to get out of Mando's grip, stopped kicking and slumped to the floor. The medical assistants lifted him to a gurney and wheeled him to the infirmary. After the commotion was over, Nina ran up to Mando.

"My hero," she said as she patted him on the shoulder.

She kissed him on the cheek, but Mando's heart was racing and he hardly noticed Nina.

Celine ran over and handed Mando a cup of water. He gulped it down.

"Are you okay?" she mumbled. He nodded yes.

"Thanks, Celine. What a party. Went out with a bang."

Nina rolled her eyes at him and Celine, then joined her sister who was watching with the astonished group.

"What was that all about?" Mr. Smith asked Dr. Vee.

Everyone was quietly waiting for Dr. Vee's response.

"Mr. Monroe, as you know, is a Sensitive and might be suffering from space sickness. I'm sure he'll be fine."

"What was he saying to you before the doctor jabbed him?" Mr. Smith asked Mando.

He said, "'They're out there. I have to open the airlock'."

Everyone gasped and turned their heads toward the large window.

"I don't see anything out there," said Mr. Smith.

"Exactly," said Dr. Vee. "Just as I said, Mr. Monroe is delirious. You can't listen to anything he says."

Celine stared out the large windows in the Commons. Dr. Vee had called Mr. Monroe a Sensitive. The Colonists had said she was sensitive. She wondered if she might get sick like Mr. Monroe. She continued to stare out the window until she could see the stars of the Milky Way. Millions of them. She also noticed the asteroid, the same cylinder-shaped rock she had seen earlier. *Strange. It seems so close. How did it get so close to us so quickly?*

Venera woke Celine from her thoughts.

"The party would have been grand if it hadn't been for Mr. Monroe," she said with a bit of disappointment in her voice. "He had emotional outbursts like that on the way to Mars. Come to think of it, it happened just as we were about two weeks out. Something about this area seems to have that effect on him."

"Poor man," said Celine. "I hope he'll be okay."

Then she glanced out the window again. There seemed to be something strange about that asteroid. She had seen many, but this one looked and behaved unnaturally. It almost seemed as if it was following them.

That night, Celine was having difficulty sleeping. She tried to make sense out of the strange things that happened since being on the spaceship. Fretfully she fell asleep.

In her dream, she heard what sounded like a chorus, and she began to mumble to herself and joined the chorus.

"We're out here. Open the airlock," she said.

CHAPTER 9

MORE THAN A KARATE LESSON

The next day Celine didn't remember her nightmare or speaking in her sleep. She only remembered the glow she felt for putting together a nearly perfect birthday party for the twins. Surely, they appreciated it. Now they would see her as a worthwhile friend. After all, putting the party together, with some help from Venera, should show them that Celine was smart and creative, but most of all caring. Celine felt it was important to prove to herself that she could make friends with anyone. Even those who don't seem to like her.

She couldn't wait to see the twins in the gym today, but before going to the gym she wanted to stop by the infirmary to check on Mr. Monroe. She felt so sorry for the poor man. She had never seen anyone treated so harshly, tackled, and held down as if he was a wild dog.

Mr. Monroe was surprised to have Celine as his first visitor; after all, he felt he had ruined her party. She assured him that he hadn't and told him she was happy to see he was in his right mind. He couldn't stop laughing after she said that, which made her wonder if she had praised his state of mind too quickly. She was relieved when his business partner entered the infirmary, giving her an excuse to leave.

"Peace and harmony to you, Mr. Monroe," she said. "And to you, sir," she said to Mr. Monroe's friend.

As she exited the infirmary quickly, she heard the men talking about her, "What a well-mannered young lady. How considerate of her to visit you."

People always had good things to say about her, and hearing this added to her joy. Celine glowed with happiness. *Today is going to be a wonderful day!* As she headed to the lady's community restroom to change into her new fitness wear, she passed the media room where she saw the teacher and Nina talking. Nina didn't seem very happy, which Celine felt was normal, but the teacher didn't seem very happy either. Which was not normal. Celine walked a little closer to the media room, but she kept walking. She didn't want anyone to think she didn't respect their privacy. She heard what sounded like the teacher telling Nina that she would have to retake her science test. The reason for retaking the test eluded her, but Celine thought the teacher was very considerate to give Nina a second chance to improve her test grade.

When Celine left the lady's room, she was wearing a crisp white jacket and loose-fitting comfortable pants. She had told Venera that Mando would be teaching her martial arts, so the beautiful kind lady printed the white uniform for her. It had a white belt, too, that Celine had tied around her waist.

"The white belt shows you are a beginner," Venera had told her as she handed her the white suit. *I wish she was my age. She would make a wonderful friend.*

Skipping through the quiet hall, Celine headed to the exercise room. She could hardly contain her joy. At last, she was beginning to feel like she was being accepted. At last, the twins would welcome her friendship. As she skipped through the spa area on a polished shiny floor, a delicate scent of lavender delightfully tickled her nose. She saw Mrs. Smith and Ms. Ballinger having tea in the garden. She smiled and waved as she skipped by. Memories of the crowded noisy halls of the Compound on Mars with its constant circulation of stale air were beginning to fade.

Today is a good day for a good day!

Mando was already in the gym when she arrived. He wore an identical white uniform, but his belt was green. He told her that he would teach her some basic Karate movements, but she would have to learn and follow the karate philosophy of living in peace and harmony, have self-control, respect for others, and with a positive attitude, strive for the best. Celine agreed. She felt like she was already following the karate philosophy.

"Karate is not just exercise," he told her. "It is a way of being. It is a way of life."

"Do the twins practice Karate?" she asked.

"They follow Kung Fu. Kung fu followers seek to live in harmony and balance with the Tao. There must be a balance between the Yin and the Yang energies."

Celine wasn't sure what that meant, and she didn't really care. She was anxious to get started with her karate lesson. She noticed the twins walking into the room. They were wearing the same uniform she and Mando wore, but their belts were black.

"Konnichiwa! (Hello!)" said Celine, and bowed her head in their direction.

She was eager to let the twins know that she was learning a lot about their culture.

Anna bowed and smiled at Celine, but Nina seemed amused. She smiled at Mando and then gave Celine the same closed-mouth smile before joining her sister on the other side of the gym.

"Let's get started," Mando said. "I will demonstrate and then you do the same. Okay?"

Celine nodded yes, but she wondered why Nina didn't seem happy to see her. *Didn't she like the party?*

Mando was waiting for her response.

"Okay," she said.

Celine bowed as he had shown her. Then he took a wide-legged stance and began bouncing back and forth, his hands held high near his face as if he was protecting it.

She imitated him and found herself enjoying the bouncing—almost like skipping.

This will make my legs even stronger. I will be ready for Earth.

The twins began their practice, which appeared to be more aggressive than what Mando was showing her. Suddenly Nina and Anna stopped their practice and began laughing and speaking in Japanese. Celine thought this was so rude since neither she nor Mando could speak the language.

"Why don't you learn Kung Fu from a real Master," Nina said to Celine. "I can teach you."

Mando's lower jaw tensed and there was a wrinkle on his forehead.

"This is not Kung Fu, Nina, and you know it," he said.

"Oh, yes. Karate. Karate's no good."

"Sister!" said Anna. She grabbed Nina's arm. "Remember what Mother said. No more trouble."

But Nina ignored her. "Defend yourself!" she shouted to Mando, who immediately jumped into a defensive stance. Nina ran over to Mando and quickly kicked him in the back of his head. He almost fell over and seemed stunned. He rubbed the back of his head and neck. Nina grinned at him.

"I did not kick your neck, but I could have. See? Karate is no good," she said as she faced Celine.

Mando's face was as red as a beet and his eyes teared up.

He turned toward Celine and said, "You can practice with them if you want." Then he headed to the door and left as Nina taunted him in Japanese and English.

"Karate's no good," Nina jeered.

That was it, Celine had had enough! She had put up with Nina making fun of her. But this time she had gone too far. Mando was doing her a favor and was being treated horribly for being her friend.

"Everyone says that they cannot tell you twins apart!" Celine shouted. "But I can! You are the ugly one!"

The moment the hateful words roared from Celine's mouth she felt a wave of sadness rush from Nina. Celine heard the painful scream in her head before it came from Nina's mouth.

It was like a powerful wave of low frequencies, leaving her breathless. She was immediately sorry she had said it. Then she saw the fiery red aura around Nina, who was rushing toward her with both hands in a fist. Celine ran for the door and then it opened, and Dr. Vee stepped in. What a relief. Nina stopped in her tracks.

"Are you girls enjoying your time on the ship?"

"Yes, thank you," Celine said as she exited the room.

Nina tried hard to hold back the tears, but she couldn't. Anna wrapped her arms around her sister to console her. She didn't know what to say. She knew that Nina felt she was the ugly twin and now Celine had confirmed it. They had been joined at birth. The doctors separated them, but Nina got the worse deal. At least that's how Nina felt. "No one will love me with this CBI (Computer-Brain-Interface)," she would say, then take off her wig and look at the metallic part of her head where no hair would grow. She called herself a Cyborg. Her mom had always assured her that no one could really tell them apart. That had always been true, but Celine had somehow seen the difference and had called her ugly. Nina laid her head on her sister's shoulder and whimpered.

That night, Nina cried silently as her sister slept. She looked at her beautifully perfect twin with her naturally thick straight hair. She patted her own head, the part where no hair would grow; the smooth metal plate that stood in place of bone. Yes, Anna and she were twins, but she had gotten the worse deal.

Her mom had always told her that no one could tell her and her sister apart. But today, Celine had called her ugly. How could she have known that she was the ugly one, the one with a CBI because part of her brain was missing, or that she was the one with the bionic eye because she was born with one eye missing? Tears flowed from her good eye.

Even so, Nina felt like Celine was just an outback, no-nothing Martian. She had no history like the Emoto family, which went back to the Shogun period, where their greatest grandfather was a Samurai, a member of the ruling class.

Even a cyborg like me is above her. One day, I will be matched with my equal. I will marry and have a normal child and Celine will return to her red, dusty, nothing of a planet.

Nina bit her lower lip and stared into the emptiness.

"No one will want me," a whisper came from her dry lips. "No one will want the ugly one. Celine, you'll be sorry you called me ugly. I promise you will regret those words."

Nina gently pulled the covers over her shoulder, closed her eyes, and cried herself to sleep.

CHAPTER 10

YOU'RE NOT MY FRIEND

I called Nina ugly. *How could I have permitted myself to get so angry? And I had just told Mando that I would follow the karate philosophy. I'm so glad he wasn't there to hear me. I should have left, as he did. It's too late now. I can't take those words back. Everything was getting better between me and the twins, but I ruined it!*

Celine decided to go to the Dome, a quiet place for reflection, to think about what she should do, to forgive herself, and to pray that Nina would also forgive her.

Dr. Vee was leaving the Dome when she entered.

"Good day," she said, remembering the good manners she had often used on Mars.

He was his usual happy self and nodded at her as he left.

Celine loved the Dome. The room was completely paneled from floor to ceiling in artificial birch wood. According to Mando, the room even had an outdoorsy scent. Though she had no idea what that meant, she loved the scent and found it relaxing.

High vibration music she understood and would play it when meditating alone in her quarters. But in the Dome, it was different. In the Dome, she could feel the vibrations of the music throughout her body. She closed her eyes and began to take deep breaths in and long exhales. Then she began her chants.

Meanwhile, outside the peaceful Dome, an emergency announcement was being made.

A class X solar storm was heading toward the ship. Suddenly the door to the Dome slid open and the emergency siren, along with Celine's Valet Bot, blasted into the room. She immediately snapped out of her alpha state. Her eyes popped open and floating above her head was her bot.

"What's happening? Are we having another drill?"

Not wasting a moment, the bot spoke with urgency in its mechanical voice.

"Solar storm! You have three minutes to get to the water room!"

"Oh no!"

She uncrossed her legs. They felt heavy and numb, but she moved as quickly as she could from the floor. Then she paused.

Her mind was now racing in confusion. *Which garden is nearby? Can my blood-deprived legs move fast enough?* Her bot must have observed her confusion.

"Follow me!" it said as it floated out the door.

First, she skipped as quickly as she could to keep up. Her bot was moving so quickly that she was afraid she might lose sight of it.

"Doors closing in 60 seconds!" came a voice on the Com system and then a countdown began.

"59, 58, 57…"

Celine willed herself to run faster than she ever had. When she saw the flower garden and Mando waiting in the doorway, she gave a sigh of relief but didn't slow down. She skipped into the garden, right past him, with only seconds to spare. She was the last one in. The door closed behind her, and she could hear it begin to fill with water.

"Solar storm?" she asked Mando once she had caught her breath.

"Highly charged energy from a solar storm has been spotted heading this way. Class X! Didn't you hear the announcement?"

The exhausted girl shook her head no.

"My Valet Bot found me and told me I had three minutes to get here, or I would be locked out."

"Well, you barely made it. Thank goodness you're safe."

The heavy water-filled door to the garden clicked, locking them in. She looked around to see who else had found safety in the flower garden. The twins were there. They were seated on a bench near the wall adjacent to the Smiths' honeymoon suite. She had avoided them since her angry outburst at Nina.

She stared in their direction, but they seemed preoccupied with something Nina was holding in her hand. She had a bunch of flowers covering it so Celine couldn't get a good look at it. Lately, the twins had been spending lots of time in the flower garden. Meditating, Mando had told her.

"They meditate every morning before breakfast and almost every night before bed."

He rubbed his hairless chin. "Interesting. Didn't think they would like that kind of thing."

Celine agreed. She remembered passing the flower garden one morning and noticing the twins were hiding behind the large rose bushes, muffling their laughter. She couldn't tell what they were doing but remembered it appeared rather suspicious.

The Smiths and Ballingers had also found refuge in the flower garden. Their premium suites were on either side of the garden, so that made sense. Mr. Abiola's suites were in the captain's hall. He had two, one for himself and a private celebrity that no one ever saw. He was standing in a corner, arms folded across his chest and staring suspiciously at everyone. He seemed to be standing in front of someone or maybe someone was deliberately standing behind him. Celine didn't care. She was just relieved she made it to the garden and was safe for now.

There was an eight-minute countdown to impact. In eight minutes, the energy from the solar flare would pass through the ship. The wait seemed like a lifetime as Celine stared at the military clock above the door. Everyone waited silently. This was the first time they had to hunker down in the garden. Tension was on everyone's faces.

However, upon impact, no one felt anything. There was a loud exhale from everyone, and the tension left their faces. An announcement crackled over the speaker.

"We are no longer in danger. You may return to your busi…"

The lights flashed and then everything went black, and the soft hum of the life-supporting machinery went silent. Men and women screamed in fear. Celine felt someone move close to her, brushing against her shoulder. Then the lights blinked a few times and came on for good. And so did the gentle hum of the life-support machinery, but no one moved. It was as if the reality of their situation was being considered.

Celine swallowed and remained still. It had been so dark she could not have seen her hands if held up in front of her face. With shaky legs, she found a bench to sit on.

"Please resume your business. Dinner will be served thirty minutes late today,"

Dr. Vee told them.

He smiled as if everything was fine, but his armpits leaked sweat that ran down his arms and off his fingertips to the floor.

Both his big and small hearts were pounding loudly. He hoped no one noticed.

Everyone silently exited the gardens except Celine and the twins, who remained seated on the far side of the room, away from Celine, next to the wall of the Smiths' suite. Celine didn't think she could eat dinner after such a scare. She thought she would stay in the safety of the garden for a while. She sat there looking at the flowers and waiting for her heart to stop pounding so quickly. Being in the dark was so scary. She remembered that the Compound had lost power a few times, but the generators had kicked in immediately and they were never in total darkness. It was not a comfortable feeling to be in total darkness, feeling oneself still moving forward through space.

Celine continued the prayers and meditation that she didn't get to finish in the Dome room. After meditating silently for twenty minutes, she could hear the twins laughing. *What could be so funny?* She could see them sitting on the floor behind the rose bushes. She tip-toed over to look. She was surprised to see that they had a set of binoculars and were looking at the wall of the Smiths' suite. They were taking turns looking and laughing.

"What are you guys doing?" she asked.

She noticed they seemed startled, and that Anna slipped the binoculars behind a large flowerpot.

"Oh! Celine, we didn't know you were still in here."

"Were you eavesdropping?" asked Nina. "You know that's against the Privacy Code."

Celine couldn't believe her ears. She was about to tell Nina what she had seen them do but decided she didn't need any more drama.

"Forget it," she said.

She went back to her bench where she had been meditating. She noticed when the girls left the garden, they did not have the binoculars with them. She decided to see if they were still behind the flowerpot, and they were. She picked them up to examine them. *Why were they staring at the wall with this?*

She put the binoculars to her eyes and looked at the wall. She could see into the Smiths' suite! They appeared to be asleep in their bed! The alarmed girl almost dropped the binoculars. *This thing is illegal. Where could they have gotten this?* She thought she would take it to Dr. Vee and report the twins right away.

She didn't notice that Nina had returned to get the binoculars and was standing in the doorway, watching her, and remembering how Celine had told her parents when she and her sister had put a hot pepper recipe in the food printer back on Mars. Nina left the garden quickly. She had a plan and she needed to act on it before Celine got them in trouble.

However, Celine took the binoculars to her Pod and put them in the drawer under her bed. She decided she didn't want to tattle on the twins after all. She remembered they had called her a tattler when she told her parents about the hot peppers. *I'll just keep them so they can't invade the Smiths' privacy again. They won't know where the binoculars are. And I'll turn them in when we reach Artemis. I'll say I found them somewhere.*

Celine was sitting in her Pod when Dr. Vee and one of the ship's administrators came marching down the sleeping hall and stopped in front of her.

"Celine, we have a complaint filed against you."

"What? Why?" Celine's eyes widened with concern.

"It has been brought to our attention that you have been abusing the Privacy Code."

The administrator's mouth was turned down in a sour manner.

"We need to search your things. Please unlock your drawer," he said.

Celine quietly did as she was told.

"I can explain," she said when the administrator used a pincher to lift the binoculars from her drawer.

"I saw Anna and Nina looking into the Smiths' suite and I brought them here. I was going to report it, but you didn't give me a chance."

"Yes, I see," said the administrator.

"Tsk," said Dr. Vee as he shook his head in pity.

Out of all the teens, she was his favorite. He was surprised and disappointed.

"Celine Red Cloud, you are formally charged with Invasion of the Privacy Code. How do you plead?" asked the administrator, spittle flying from his full lips onto Celine's jumpsuit.

"What? I'm innocent. I haven't done anything wrong."

"You are confined to your Pod until this matter has been resolved," he said.

Celine looked down at her feet. She remembered her parents telling her to not let the twins get her in trouble. Now she was in the worst trouble ever.

"I will let you know when we are ready for your hearing," said Dr. Vee gently.

"Oh no. My parents…"

"They will be informed," he said.

Then both men left with the binoculars in a clear bag. It all happened so quickly.

Celine, in tears, called Venera.

"I need you," she said between sniffles. "Something awful has happened." Celine could hardly speak.

"I'll be right there," said Venera.

In a matter of minutes, Venera was there to comfort Celine. Between coughs and sniffles, the bewildered teen explained what happened.

"You shouldn't have touched them, and when you did you should have gone directly to Dr. Vee."

Celine nodded. "I know. I know."

"When is your hearing?"

Celine sighed. "Dr. Vee said they will call me."

"Well, they'll have to examine the binoculars. The twins' fingerprints should be on them, too."

"That's no help. They'll just say we were in this together. My parents will be so disappointed," Celine whimpered.

"I'm so sorry, Celine."

Venera wrapped her arm around the shoulders of her sad protégé.

"May I go to the hearing with you?"

"Would you please." Tears rolled down Celine's face.

"Let me know when they are ready. I'll be there for you."

An hour later Celine's Valet Bot came to show her to the hearing room. It floated ahead of her, and she walked slowly behind it. She felt like everyone knew and was watching her.

She followed the bot into a small room next to the media room. She thought it had been used for storage because she never saw anyone go in there. Dr. Vee was waiting at the entrance hall and told her to sit up front before the large green screen.

"Venera said she will be with me for the hearing," she told him.

"She's been informed."

Just then the door opened and Venera and the twins walked in. Venera came over to join Celine and the twins were instructed to sit on the opposite side of the room, but also facing the green screen.

A hologram that looked like a lanky black man wearing a curly white wig appeared in front of the screen.

"Hear ye. Hear ye. The honorable Judge Emoto presiding. All, rise."

Instantly the hologram changed into a large round-faced man who looked like he could have been the twins' uncle. Everyone in the room stood up.

Celine looked at the hologram and then at Venera. "All hope is lost," she said.

Venera looked at Celine. "This is all new to me," she said.

Celine told the hologram everything that happened. She even told why she didn't want to get the twins in trouble. She could not tell if he was listening or merely waiting for her to shut up so he could pronounce her guilty.

"Do you have any proof?" Judge Emoto asked.

"No, I do not, sir."

"Then I have no recourse. You are guilty of code 333, Invasion of Privacy Code. Your parents, Mr. and Mrs. Red Cloud, and your mother, Ms. Abbie Voltaire, are fined a total of 3,000 credits."

"Oh no. You can't do that. That's not fair."

"You are dismissed," said the hologram. Then it disappeared.

"Is that it? This is supposed to be a fair trial?" asked Venera.

Celine sat speechless. She only thought of all those credits her parents would have to pay.

Dr. Vee said, "I'm so sorry, Celine. I listened to your testimony. I believe you, but I had no right to intercede with the law. You understand."

No, I don't, she wanted to say. But she did not want to be disrespectful.

"I'll walk you out," he said.

Celine and Venera headed to the door together. As they were leaving Celine noticed Nina's close-lipped smile. Celine gasped. *You did this to me.*

Dr. Vee stepped into the hall with them.

"May I get a new Pod? I don't want to stay next to the twins," Celine asked him.

"I'll see what I can do." His usual jolly face seemed sad.

As he went back into the Hearing Room, Celine could see the hearing continue.

"Hear ye. Hear ye," said the lanky caller. All rise for the honorable Judge Red Cloud presiding." And in seconds the judge's image appeared, looking like her dad.

"Oh my," heaved Celine and she ran down the hall, leaving Venera at the door. By the time she had reached her Pod, anger had grabbed hold of her like an animal trapped in a dark abyss. She wanted to scream, but what good would that do? *I'm going to pay them back for what they did to me. I'm putting artificial snakes, and spiders, and every nasty thing I can think of in their Pod. I'll make them sorry they've ever met me.*

Venera caught up with Celine at her Pod.

"Are you going to be all right?" she asked.

"Yes, I'm going to pack my things. I can't stay here."

Venera gave Celine a hug.

"I don't need a hug. I want my good name back. Everyone will think I'm a Peeping Tom. That's not who I am. And my parents will have to pay an extra tax that they cannot afford. They need that for my new baby brother."

"I know. We'll find a way to make this right. Okay?"

Celine nodded. "Okay."

After Venera left, Celine opened her drawer and took out her outdoor jumpsuit, Robo pug, glass computer, and flute. She piled them on her bed.

"That's it," she sighed. "That's all I have. And I don't care!"

She cried until she had no more tears, but beneath the sadness was a wave of anger she had never known, frighteningly intense. She picked up her flute, hoping to calm herself, but was too angry to play it. As she stared out the window at the end of the sleeping hall, plotting her revenge, she noticed the cylinder-shaped asteroid.

There it is again. She sniffled. *Oh well. Not my problem. I'm sure Dr. Vee has some administrator who can handle that.*

Later that day, one of the employees agreed to exchange Pods with Celine. She preferred the new Pod because she couldn't see the twins. She wouldn't even have to pass them in the hall. She trembled with rage and then felt disappointed that she didn't turn the binoculars in right away.

That night as Celine tossed about and mumbled to herself, the blue shadow stood next to her Pod and didn't leave until she started mumbling in her sleep.

"We're out here. Open the door," she mumbled.

The blue shadow walked away, quickly heading towards the captain's suites.

CHAPTER 11

NIGHTMARES

The next morning Celine felt awful.

"I didn't sleep well," she told Mando as she rubbed the back of her neck.

"I didn't either," he said. "I felt like I was being watched and you kept mumbling. It sounded like you were having a nightmare."

"I'm living my nightmare," Celine said, referring to her ordeal with Judge Emoto.

"I heard about it. I'm so sorry."

She wasn't surprised he knew. She thought everyone on the spaceship would know sooner or later. *Bad news travels fast.*

"I suppose everyone will think I'm awful," she said.

She stared at Mando, hoping to read his response.

"I don't think anyone could possibly think you're a bad person. You're one of the most innocent people I know."

Celine felt she could see the sincerity in his face.

"What really happened?" he asked.

He patted the empty space on his bed next to him.

"Sit down. You can talk with me about it."

She plopped down on the bed next to him.

"I don't want to talk about it right now. I just know I don't want to be friends with the twins anymore. They're horrible human beings."

Mando bit his lip and exhaled.

"I'm sorry to hear that," he said.

He continued, "Um, Nina asked me to be her boyfriend."

Celine quickly moved from slouching to sitting upright.

"She asked what?" Celine said in disbelief. "Didn't she kick you in the head a few days ago?"

Mando didn't respond to the question but sat there with a silly grin on his face. Celine crossed her arms in front of her chest, waiting for a response but getting none.

"And what did you say?" she finally asked. The uncomfortable look on Mando's face told her she didn't really want to hear the answer.

"Well, she is kind of pretty," he murmured.

"Unbelievable! Pretty? Yes, but she has such ugly ways! That nullifies any beauty you can see in her face."

"Well, I like her."

"She insulted you! And I defended you."

"But that's all in the past. She apologized to me, and I accepted it."

"Well, she hasn't apologized for mistreating me, and if she does, I won't accept it!"

Celine couldn't believe she was speaking in such a negative manner, that she was still holding on to the anger she had for the twins as if the anger would make things right.

Then, as if summoned, the twins entered the sleeping hall.

"Nina," said Mando as they entered the hall.

When Celine saw them, she quickly turned her face away from them, stood up and marched down the opposite hall without looking back. Mando didn't bother to call her either, and now she felt she had no friends.

What happened to my dream of having three friends by the time I reach Earth? I hate them. I hate them all.

She marched to the media room where one of the three-dimensional printers could be used. After a bit of research, she was able to code and print designs for several unpleasant critters: black widow spiders, scorpions, and pincher bugs, all with movable legs. She even created a baby armadillo to throw in with the plastic arachnids and insects, just to make a point. She created a small bag for the little critters, gathered them up, and dropped them into the bag.

"I'll fix them," she mumbled, and headed for the door just as Mr. Smith entered. It was an awkward moment for Celine and Mr. Smith.

"Good day," she said and held her bag of critters behind her back.

He smiled with his lips closed and nodded to acknowledge her.

Mr. Smith then headed to the printer and was surprised to see a small plastic scorpion behind the machine as he was about to use it.

"Did you leave this?" he called and held the arachnid up by its tail before Celine could leave the room. She ran back to get it.

"For a science project," she said and snatched the scorpion from his hand, then dropped it into her bag.

"Thank you."

Oh, my. I don't recognize myself.

She didn't like lying to anyone, but she couldn't very well tell Mr. Smith that she was about to break the Privacy Code again, even though she never did. Revenge was calling her name and this time she would heed its call.

She headed for her Pod but stopped in her tracks when she saw the blue shadow standing alone in front of the small window in an isolated section of the ship. She was determined to go right up to it and touch it. She didn't care what that touch might lead to. Maybe the blue shadow would be her friend.

Moving as quickly as she could, she rushed toward it. The shadow jerked as though startled, then began to run towards the Commons ahead of her, as if running from her. As she sped behind it, her legs began to feel heavy and she couldn't keep up. She reached the Commons in time to see the shadow merge with Mr. Abiola.

She wanted to run up to Mr. Abiola, beat him on his chest, and say 'I know what you're hiding', but he was big and scary. Besides, Dr. Vee might call the medics to give her a hypo in front of everyone. She couldn't bear the thought of more humiliation.

Mr. Abiola looked at her and smiled. Celine quickly turned her head away. She could not bear to look into his eyes; having one brown and the other turquoise was disarming.

He should be wearing contacts like mine.

Venera noticed Celine and called her over to see the Breaking News.

"I have some things I need to put in my Pod. I'll return later," said Celine, not wanting to explain what was in her bag.

When she arrived at the sleeping hall, she found herself alone and thought this might be the perfect time to throw the critters into the twins' sleeping Pod. She pushed the button labeled open, but nothing happened. Usually, they didn't bother to lock their Pod. Fortunately for them, today they had. The angry girl decided she would wait for that opportunity to give them their deserved surprise. She put her bag in her drawer next to her sleeping pug and locked it. She rushed back to the

Commons to see why everyone was watching the large media screen.

She entered the room unnoticed.

"The Europa Clipper 3 has finally landed on Europa!" said the news reporter on the large media screen. "What an exciting day for all of humanity!"

"Oh my gosh!" Celine shouted, causing several hush sounds from some of the viewers.

She had been so overwhelmed by the turn of events in her life that she had forgotten all about the astronauts landing on one of Jupiter's seventy-nine moons today. This had been talked about for months when Celine was on Mars. Most of the colonists expected the Clipper astronauts to discover some form of life on Europa.

"Come join me. The news has just started," said Venera to Celine.

As Celine sat with Venera she thought, *At least I do have one friend, even if she's twice my age.*

"Do you think they'll find life there?" she asked Venera.

"Of course not," yelled Nina, who was sitting with her sister and new boyfriend, Mando.

"There're no little green men out there. Have you ever seen any on Mars?" She laughed.

Celine ignored Nina. What Nina said to her or about her no longer mattered.

Venera said, "I believe they will find life, but will they tell us? I don't believe so."

Mr. Smith looked at Venera in disbelief.

"You see, that's the problem with young people. Older folks are always telling them what they want to hear," he said.

Then Mr. Ballinger joined the conversation.

"There are at least two trillion galaxies in the universe, and you think we humans are the only intelligent beings? And I do use the word intelligent with reservation."

"Well, partner, I'm willing to bet a million credits that they will not find anything on that there moon. You want to put your credits where your mouth is?"

"Of course not. You know I'm not a gambler."

The two men continued to push their arguments, giving the pros and cons for the existence of extraterrestrials. Mr. Smith said no one has given any solid evidence that aliens exist, and he had never seen one. Mr. Ballinger said he should do the math like Celine did in her debate. "With over two trillion galaxies, over two hundred billion stars, and some like our sun with planets orbiting them, you know some must be in the Goldilocks Zone."

"In what zone?" Mr. Smith laughed. He looked at his wife. "You hear that, honey? The man's talking about little children's stories."

"I give up!" said Mr. Ballinger and shook his head. "It's a good thing you inherited," he mumbled.

"Be nice," whispered Mrs. Ballinger to her husband.

Venera and Celine giggled.

"I think you started something, Celine."

"Hush, everyone," Dr. Vee said with a smile directed at Mr. Abiola.

Mr. Abiola winked at Dr. Vee. Celine noticed that quick interplay between the two friends and wondered why it had happened. Not knowing what to think of it, she redirected her attention to the media screen. The reporter for the World Space Program continued talking about the ten astronauts who had been selected; each of Earth's six continents was represented by them.

Earth is so diverse, Celine thought. It would be difficult for her to live there for two years, but she would do what she must, with or without friends.

Meanwhile on Europa, a female astronaut from Nigeria and a male astronaut from the USA took the first steps on the icy moon for humanity. They were followed by astronauts from China, Brazil, Japan, the Arab Republic, and the European Alliance. As they sat instruments down to study the thick ice and the water below it, they heard and felt the vibrations of something moving under the ice, heading in their direction. To their surprise, there appeared to be hundreds of single-celled animals in the water. They were as large as the helmets the astronauts were wearing. They were colorless and seemed to have the consistency of a gel.

"They behave like amoeba," said one of the astronauts. "Look! More are coming."

"That could be dangerous," said the captain. "We'll need to return to the ship immediately. I'll inform World Space and wait for further instructions."

After the astronauts shared their findings with World Space, it was decided that further study would be needed to determine if what the astronauts saw were life forms.

"These could be large gas bubbles that we are not familiar with," said one of the scientists in the Command Center on Earth. "No need to create a worldwide panic."

His comrades agreed. The astronauts were told to continue collecting data on the phenomena from the safety of the ship, and if the ship was threatened, they should go into orbit immediately.

Then the World Space news reporter announced in his most convincing voice that no life had been found on Jupiter's moon. He continued his broadcast, showing beautiful photos of the icy moon from a distance. He even threw in a few interesting photos of the huge red spot on Jupiter.

"About one thousand three hundred Earths could fit into that large red spot," he said, sharing news that was hundreds of years old.

On the Fantasy, Mr. Smith listened with satisfaction. He had heard exactly what he wanted to hear from the World Space Program's reporter.

"See, I told you they wouldn't find anything. You're lucky you're not a gambler. Ha-ha!" Mr. Smith said to Mr. Ballinger, who set his cold drink on one the elegant tables and left the Commons. Both Mrs. Smith and Mrs. Ballinger shook their heads and smiled at each other.

Nina gave a self-satisfied grin at Celine, who looked straight past her at the blue shadow that was leaving the Commons.

Celine jumped up and headed toward the shadow, but again Mr. Abiola rushed to block her. Dr. Vee could see a confrontation coming. He ran over to Celine to let her know that it was her turn to call her parents on Mars.

Hearing that felt like a thud in her chest, because she did not want to talk with her parents. She knew that they would ask her about the case and the fine. She'd have to tell them how silly she was to take the binoculars and hide them among her things.

"Celine," said Dr. Vee gently. "I know you don't want to talk to them about what happened today, but they have already received the fine. I'll join you if you need me to speak with them about it."

"No, that won't be necessary. I can deal with…" Celine's voice drifted off.

Reluctantly, she walked slowly to the Media Room to call her parents. She felt so horrible explaining how she had gotten into trouble just because she didn't turn the binoculars in right away because she wanted to keep the twins from getting into trouble. She promised her dad that she would repay him the credits and was shocked to learn that Alex had already paid the fine.

"How did he know about it?" Celine asked, her throat tightening. She wondered who else knew that she had caused her parents such trouble.

"I don't know. I didn't speak with him. It was in the invoice that it was paid for by Alex Rittenhouse."

Celine wanted to scream, but she remained calm. "I'm in the data," she mumbled, and then changed the topic quickly to prevent an explosion of tears.

"How is Hannah?" she asked as she tried to hide her anger from her dad.

"I'm fine," said her stepmom from the background. Celine could see Hannah holding her new baby brother! "But how are you, Celine?" she asked.

"Oh, he's so cute," Celine said, ignoring Hannah's question. Hannah sighed. Celine continued, happy to be distracted by all that cuteness on her Com screen.

"Are you still going to name him Ceres after that large asteroid in the Asteroid Belt?"

"No, we haven't named him yet." Hannah paused. "You are okay, aren't you?"

"I'm okay. I wish I was still on Mars, though. I could be holding my brother instead of dealing with all this madness." Celine fought to hold back the tears. "He'll be two years old and walking by the time I get to see him."

"I'll send lots of photos and videos," said Hannah.

"Just don't get into any more trouble," said her dad.

"I won't," Celine said.

"Love you," said her dad and stepmom in unison.

"Love you, too. I'll call you next week."

The Com screen went white, and Celine slumped back into her chair. Now the idea of revenge didn't feel so tempting. After seeing how supportive her parents were, she couldn't afford to get into any more trouble. She went to her Pod to get the insects. She decided she would break them into small unrecognizable pieces and put them into the recycle bin next to the 3-D printer. When she opened the drawer of her storage unit, her pug jumped up to lick her face. A plastic armadillo's leg dropped from her pug's mouth. All the plastic insects were gone. Celine burst into laughter. "Puggie, you're my little hero, aren't you? You weren't going to let me do something bad."

Meanwhile, in Dr. Vee's suite, Dr. Vee had placed a bland meal of oatmeal and a baby's bottle of goat's milk on his dining table. Earlier he had missed his breakfast and lunch and was famished. He opened his shirt and rolled down his pants to uncover his navel which was opened wide as a small mouth. He shoved a spoonful of oatmeal directly into his stomach through the navel opening and it began a toothless chew.

After much slurping and gumming, the bowl of oatmeal was emptied of every morsel. Dr. Vee then shoved the nipple of the bottle of goats' milk directly into his navel and it began to nurse, making a sucking sound as it emptied the bottle.

Normally, he ate like the humans from Earth, but when he missed a meal or two he would eat like the humans from his home world, a large planet located 4.4 light years from Earth.

As he rubbed his swollen belly, he thought of how strange it was that some of Earth's humans thought they were the only humans in the universe. He considered himself to be human, even though he was from a distant world. His parents had traveled to this solar system to live among and observe Earth's humans. He and his brothers were born on Earth's moon and though they could be officially called Earthlings, they knew they were not.

One day, he and his brother would get the opportunity to visit their home world, where they would find wives and return to Earth, to take his parents' place as observers. Thoughts of Mr. Smith and his ignorance made Dr. Vee sigh.

"I wonder when all of Earth's people will be ready to know about my kind," he mumbled.

His thoughts were interrupted by the door buzzer, and he quickly fastened his shirt to hide his belly, threw his beautiful cape over his shoulders, and went to his door. He opened it and was pleasantly surprised to see his friend Mr. Abiola waiting to speak with him.

"Ah! Come in my friend."

CHAPTER 12

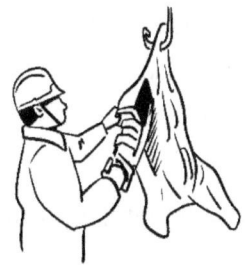

SO, THIS IS A MEAT LAB

The next day, everyone was still talking about the miraculous landing on Europa. Celine was relieved that they were not talking about her. She joined Venera for breakfast.

"I feel so badly about the Smiths. I want to say something to them, but I don't know what to say. I know they think I'm an awful person."

"You might be overthinking this, Celine. Everyone here knows how kind you are. Just tell them you're sorry about what happened."

"I'm sorry that happened to them, but I'm innocent."

"Tell them that. I'd think they would want to know."

When the Smiths came into the Commons, Celine headed in their direction to give them her side of the story. But as she got closer to the couple, she noticed that Mrs. Smith's aura turned a bright red, indicating to Celine that Mrs. Smith was still very angry. Celine quickly detoured for the cold foods cart where she piled a clean plate with super greens and globs of blue cheese dressing. When she returned to her table, Venera asked her what she had said to the Smiths.

"Uh, I decided that speaking to them might not be a good idea."

"Oh Celine, why not?"

Knowing that she was not going to tell Venera that Mrs. Smith's aura had turned red, Celine simply shrugged her shoulders. *I don't know.*

"There's a counselor on this ship. I've seen her a few times and I think she's pretty good. Maybe she could give you some ideas about how to deal with this situation. I know it's been very traumatic for you." Venera paused with a sigh.

"I'm okay." Celine gently touched Venera's hand. "Don't worry about me. Everything will be better in the morning."

However, Celine didn't believe her own words because every time she thought about her trial, she felt anger. No! She felt rage toward the twins.

Why did they do this to me? What have I done to make them treat me so badly?

"I've got some research to finish for my job. How about you? Do you have any plans for today? We could do a movie later, if you'd like."

"No thank you. I've already registered for the Meat Lab tour. That should keep me busy, take my mind off of everything," Celine mumbled.

Venera chuckled.

"Why on Earth would you want to visit a Meat Lab?

"We don't have real meat at home, and I've never seen one. Besides, it's just something to do."

"Well, if you must go, go with a friend. I wouldn't do the Meat Lab tour alone."

"I don't have any friends on this ship."

Venera gasped.

"At least not any friends my age. I'm ok with that. I can take Puggie."

"I don't think that's a good idea."

"He's a good friend. He's loyal and he's cute."

"But he thinks he's a real dog. I don't think the meat engineer would like it.

I'll see you later. And Celine, think seriously about talking to the ship's counselor. It's not healthy to harbor anger."

Just then, Nina and Mando came into the Commons. They were holding hands and smiling at each other.

"You see how happy they look," said Venera. "Anger hurts you, not them."

Celine's Valet Bot entered the Commons and floated toward her. Still angry, Celine lashed out at it.

"I don't need you to show me where the Meat Lab is! In fact, I don't need you for anything!

Celine's bot halted in midair, which caused it to emit a high pitch squeak from stopping so quickly. Everyone in the Commons turned to see what was happening, staring at Celine and her bot, who looked at all of the staring faces, then bolted into the hall with her bot floating behind her.

"You have a call in the Media Room from Alex Rittenhouse," the bot said once it had caught up with her.

"Alex! Why didn't you say so!" Celine scolded.

Alex was her one true friend, and the only person besides her dad who could get her in a cheerful mood. She rushed off to the Media Room and flicked on the Com.

"Alex. Where are you? Are you still on the moon? When can I send you the shows? I need the credits now!" she said in one breath.

Alex paused before replying, "What's happening with you? Are you okay?"

"Oh, Alex, you know," Celine cried, referring to her ordeal with the judge. "It's the Emoto twins. They hate me and all I've done is try to be their friend."

She proceeded to tell him the entire story about finding the binoculars and hiding them to keep the twins out of trouble.

"I didn't do anything wrong—just stupid." Celine looked down at her hands; she couldn't look at Alex on the Com screen. "My parents told me that you paid the fine. You can take the credits out of my show's royalties."

"Oh, I won't do that. I don't need those credits."

"Thanks, Alex. But I won't feel right about this until you have been repaid."

"If you insist."

"I do," Celine laughed.

"It's good to see a smile on your face. Don't worry about the Emotos. When you reach Earth, you will have plenty of friends. You'll see. I'll call you tomorrow."

The media screen went white. Celine noticed her heartbeat had slowed and she felt calm.

She now had something good to look forward to, Alex's call. Later that day, Celine took her pug from the drawer. She patted his head.

"You're a good dog, Puggie," she said as she fed him a small energy packet. As she watched him eating and wagging its short tail, she imagined him gobbling up the plastic insects. She chuckled.

After turning off her dog, she apologized to her Valet Bot. It didn't matter that it was not considered to be a sentient being. She felt it was the right thing to do.

"I won't need your help today," she said. "Why don't you sit next to my Pod and rest."

"Bots don't need rest," it said rather awkwardly. "But I will sit next to your Pod and begin running a scan. I might find data to help prove your innocence."

"Oh! I certainly wasn't expecting that." She patted her bot's round head. "Thank you," she said.

When Celine stepped into the small Meat Lab, a peculiar odor engulfed her. It was the unfamiliar scent of raw meat. A meat engineer met her at the door. He had on a white jumpsuit and apron that had a few red stains on it.

"Welcome," he said. "You are one of the few people who opted to take this tour."

"Oh. I wonder why."

The meat engineer smiled and said, "This is one of the top-o-the- line Meat Labs. First, you'll get to see the aquarium."

He directed Celine over to a tank of water. The back side appeared to be painted blue and there were colorful rocks on its bottom. Some of the rocks appeared to be releasing bubbles in the water and making a gurgling sound. The tank was full of glistening fish.

"Watch this," said the engineer. He took a scoop of food from the large bag on the floor next to the aquarium and dumped it into the tank. Celine got closer to the tank and watched the fish gulp down the food. She giggled.

"May I feed them?"

"Sure." The engineer gave Celine a smaller scoop of food which she emptied into the tank of waiting fish. They quickly nibbled the food.

"Oh, look at them. So beautiful," she said.

"Yes, I agree," said the engineer, happy that Celine had an appreciation for his work.

He showed her the fish hatchery and then gave an unexpected history lesson about how meat was produced in factory farming of cows and pigs. "Now no mammals are raised for food. All meats are grown from animal stem cells in a Meat Lab almost as good as this." He put on a white overcoat and face mask and gave Celine a coat and mask to put on before they entered a cold room called the freezer. There, he showed her large chunks of meat twitching in a red solution.

"Is it alive?" Celine asked.

"Only to a low degree. These muscle cells were taken from a living animal. That's a nutrient bath." He pointed to the thick red liquid.

"Does it hurt them?" she asked.

"Have you ever had a blood test?"

Celine nodded.

"For the animals, it's similar to a blood test."

"I don't like getting a blood test."

The meat engineer smiled.

"Believe me. If they had lived during the olden days, things would be a lot worse for them. Now farmers keep a small number of animals. The animals have free range to eat grass and humane treatment. None are killed."

"That's good to know," Celine whispered. "My dad says I should eat meat only once a day and one day a week, eat none."

"Your dad is a wise man."

"Yes, he is. Thanks," she said proudly.

"Before the meat is placed in the nutrient bath, it's placed in one of these, a bioreactor." He pointed to a box.

"It looks like an old-fashioned microwave," he said. "The cells grow in the bioreactor until there are scaffoldings. Then the scaffoldings are placed in the nutrient baths." He paused contemplatively. "Meat Labs are expensive. I understand that on Mars, most of your foods are synthetic."

"Yes. Maybe one day we could get a meat lab—one as nice as yours."

"Thank you," he said, appreciative of the teen's kind words.

"Thank you for the tour and the lesson."

"The pleasure is all mine."

"What a thoughtful young lady," was the last thing Celine heard when she left the Meat Lab. It warmed her heart. *At least some of the people on this ship still see me as a decent human being.*

Just as Celine left the Meat Lab, Nina and Anna rounded the corner. They stopped when they saw her. Anna smiled with a closed mouth, but Nina rolled her eyes and hissed before saying loud enough for everyone to hear,

"Look who just came out of that disgusting Meat Lab. See, sister, everything I told you about her is true; she's nothing but a low life."

Celine had never heard those words used to describe a person.

"What do you mean?" she fired back.

"You heard me," shouted Nina, who was always ready to release her anger on any willing victim. "Anyone who visits a Meat Lab or an undertaker is a low-life. Beneath me, and you certainly don't deserve to be our friend."

"You know nothing about me. And as for the man who works in that lab, he has more character and kindness than the two of you put together. And furthermore, you're not worthy to be my friend."

She stomped away before either of the flabbergasted twins could say a word.

CHAPTER 13

DROWNING IN MY SPACE SUIT

That night, Celine tossed and turned in her bed. Her pug laid asleep beside her, but it brought her no comfort. She was having a scary dream. In it, someone was pleading for help. Though she was not fully awake, the sleep-deprived girl began to imitate the voice she heard.

"Help me. I'm out here," she said out loud and then she sat up as if in a trance.

"I'll try," she mumbled.

She stumbled out of bed and was determined to get to the engineer repair room. She remembered the door to the engineering bridge that surrounded the ship was in that room. Maybe someone was trapped outside on the bridge. She needed to find out. As her pug lay snoring in her bed, Celine opened her Pod and silently left the sleeping hall, leaving her Pod open, which under normal circumstances she would never do. As if she was guided by a supernatural force, she found her way to the engineer's repair room. At the door, she pushed in the letters RAY and the door opened. The on-duty security man was asleep, his head resting on his desk.

Without noticing him, Celine walked right past him into the sanitizing room and began putting on a radiation suit she had seen the engineer use. She checked her oxygen level and water level as she always did when she was on Mars. She couldn't understand why she was doing this, she only knew she needed to dress quickly and help the person who was calling her.

In her haste, she didn't push the button to seal the cooling water in the suit, nor did she inhale from the oxygen tank before putting on her helmet. She pushed in the codes she had seen the engineer use to open the airlock without an alarm. Then she tethered herself to the outside of the spaceship and closed the door behind her.

Once outside, the pleading voice became louder, drawing her to the far side of the ship. "Please, help me."

Like a Bot following its master, Celine blindly followed the voice. Whoever was calling for help, sounded desperate, and Celine knew she had to find and help this person.

She shuffled forward on the bridge, totally unaware of how narrow the bridge was and how a misstep could have her dangling from the starship as it moved through deep space. Once she reached the other side of the ship, she saw the cylinder-shaped asteroid unusually close to the Fantasy. And it sounded like the plea for help was coming from the asteroid. Though it made no sense to her that someone would be on an asteroid, she felt compelled to find a way to get on it. It seemed so close that she could jump to it but could she and remained tethered to the Fantasy.

"Help me. Please. Hurry."

Startled into action, Celine began to quickly pull on the tether, drawing the extra cable next to her feet. As she looked down, she felt something cold and wet tickle her nose. She noticed the shield in her helmet began to fog up and it seemed more difficult to breathe.

She inhaled deeply, then gasped and began to cough. She had inhaled water. Immediately she snapped out of the hypnotic trance, and looked down at her covered hands, and arms.

"Why am I wearing an EVA suit?"

She looked past her feet and saw nothing but black space beneath the bridge she was standing on.

"Great Spirit! How did I get here?"

Gone were the cries for help and the asteroid that had shadowed the Fantasy.

She could only hear her heart pounding as she stood there trembling, trying to get her thoughts together. Strangely, there was a pool of water inside her helmet that covered her neck and chin and the water, though slowly, appeared to be rising. A sigh came from her throat when she remembered what she had been told about getting water in the helmet.

The water's not sealed in.

She looked down at the buttons on the sleeves. She dared not touch any of them for fear she could make things worse. Then she noticed she was tethered to the ship. That was a plus. At least she wouldn't go floating into space.

Stay Calm. The mic. It's underwater.

"This is Celine. Can anyone hear me? I need help."

There was no response. Then she noticed the lights coming from some of the nearby suites. She thought if she headed for the lights, she might be able to get someone's attention. She began to slowly inch her way toward the closest light, but before she could reach it the light went out.

Stay calm. Someone will help me.

She could now feel the water steady against her top lip.

I've got to get into the ship quickly, or I'm going to …. She couldn't say it.

To say it was to confirm it, she believed that somehow, she was going to get back in that ship. She was going to live.

I'm too young to die. Only old people die.

The words choked in her throat. Her eyes teared up and a tear drop added to the puddle of water forming in her helmet. She moved as quickly as she dared, as water gently sloshed in her helmet.

Suddenly, she could see something shiny floating toward her.

"Space junk!" she hissed and pressed her back against the starship and prayed the junk would miss her. She closed her eyes and waited.

Would the junk be jagged? Would it cut through her space suit, or would it just hit her with such force that her tether snapped loose, and she'd float out into space? She waited for the possible impact, but then she heard the most beautiful mechanical voice she'd ever heard. Her Bot.

"You must return to the ship," it said.

"Thank the Great Spirit you'll here! There's water in my helmet."

The bot floated in for a closer look.

"I must get you inside the ship quickly," it said.

Before Celine could say anything, her bot had extended its two arm-like appendages under the padded arms of her spacesuit and lifted her several feet above the bridge. She instinctively wrapped her arms around its round head.

"Can you see which way to go?"

"I know which way to go," it said as it followed the bridge back to the airlock.

When the door opened, she could hear her pug barking in the background.

"The dog was barking and awakened everyone," said her Bot. "It led me to the engineering room and I saw you on the monitor," were the last words she heard before blacking out and sliding onto the floor of the sanitizing room.

A doctor quickly unfastened and removed her helmet and water poured out on the floor.

"It's coolant water," the engineer said to the doctor.

An oxygen mask was quickly fastened around Celine's nose.

All usual safety protocol was forgotten as the large radiation suit was removed and left on the floor. Attached to the back of it was a tiny, small insect. It buzzed past security, dropping speckles of asteroid dust as it flapped its tiny wings, heading for the fruit and vegetable garden. Its tiny eyes, full of mechanical compound lenses, recorded everything it saw.

Celine was rushed to the infirmary, where she was rolled into a makeshift hyperbaric chamber, made of clear plastic. In the chamber, she could hear the oxygen quickly hissing in. Then she felt heavy pressure in her ears as though her eardrums would explode. Her hands rushed to cover both of her ears and she twisted uncomfortably on the gurney.

She heard the doctor say, "Take deep breaths, Celine. Relax. You're going to be okay."

She began to take deep breaths and slow exhales and found relief in doing this.

"I'm going to be okay," she sighed. "But I'm so tired."

"Get some rest," the doctor said. "You are one lucky girl."

After two hours in the hyperbaric chamber, she was placed on a regular bed to continue her recovery. When she awoke, Alex was standing next to her bed and Mr. Abiola appeared to be guarding the door.

"How are you feeling?" said Alex. "You gave everyone a real scare."

Celine was still groggy but looked up adoringly at her hero who had come to the infirmary to see her.

"Alex, you're here. Are we on the moon already?

Alex hesitated, then bit his lower lip. "No, we're not on the moon yet."

"You're on The Fantasy? But how? I know your dad's spaceship is fast, but didn't you tell me he had sold it to Earth's Space Force?"

Mr. Abiola raised an eyebrow and cleared his throat.

Celine looked in his direction and wondered why he was there.

"Mr. Abiola?

"I can explain," said Alex as he looked sheepishly at Mr. Abiola and then Celine.

Even though Celine had not fully recovered, she was able to put the pieces together. She looked at Mr. Abiola.

"Alex is the celebrity you were guarding?" she asked Mr. Abiola.

Mr. Abiola remained silent. Alex spoke up.

"Yes, I am."

Celine's thoughts were racing.

"I was wearing camouflage."

"But why? Were you hiding from me? I don't understand. Why didn't you tell me you were on theFantasy?"

"I couldn't. No one was supposed to know I was here. My dad didn't want me to return to Mars, but I had to. So, I wore camouflage. Besides, you weren't supposed to be here."

"But I am, and I saw you. You looked like a spooky blue shadow alien ET scaring me out of my mind!"

"I'm sorry. Normal people can't see me when I'm camouflaged. I guess I forgot how special your eyes are."

"So, you were going to visit Mars and not even visit me?"

Alex gave a long exhale. "I know this sounds awful, but I had to keep my visit to Mars a secret."

"But now you don't."

Celine didn't know how to take this information. On the one hand, she was glad to see Alex cared enough to come out of hiding to see her, and on the other hand, she was angry and saddened that he didn't think he could share his secret with her.

"The robot found you outside. Security said you appeared to be sleepwalking," Alex said, changing the subject.

"I remember breathing in water and seeing darkness all around me." Celine shivered. "It was awful."

"Well, you're safe now. Security wants to keep you in the infirmary. They're afraid you might sleepwalk again."

She looked down. She was afraid to tell him that she heard someone calling for help.

I guess I have a secret now.

"Don't worry. You won't have to stay here. I'm giving you my suite. It has the best security on the ship. Mr. Abiola and I can share his suite. It's at the entrance to the Captain's hall. No one will get past Mr. Abiola."

When Alex and Mr. Abiola left, Celine couldn't stop thinking about how Alex had hidden, and avoided her on the spaceship.

I thought I at least had a friend in Alex. But for over two months, I didn't know where he was. And he was right here, hiding under camouflage all this time. I couldn't even enjoy the trip because I thought I was having space hallucinations! And I disliked Mr. Abiola for doing his job! Alex Rittenhouse, I am very disappointed with you.

The doctor entered, breaking her train of thoughts.

"Have you ever had problems sleepwalking?" he asked.

"No, not ever."

"I understand you've been under a lot of stress recently. I heard about your trial."

Celine looked down at her hands, She felt ashamed even though she had not done what she was accused of.

"We have a great counselor on board. I recommend that you see her."

"I will."

"Great. I will set up your appointment."

"Thank you."

"Alex Rittenhouse has offered his suite which comes with security. If you accept his offer, you won't have to sleep in the infirmary. You can come back here for two more treatments in the chamber, and you'll be fine."

"I don't know if I want his suite."

The doctor crinkled his brow.

"Think about it and let me know your decision tomorrow."

"Okay."

"Also, you have another visitor waiting to see you."

"Venera?" Celine asked excitedly.

"No, a young man named Mando. Do you feel like seeing him?"

"Yeah, for a little while."

"I'll send him in."

The doctor left, and within seconds Mando was walking into the room. His eyes were watery and red. He began apologizing to Celine for how he had treated her since Nina became his girlfriend, totally ignoring her.

"From now on, I'll be here for you."

"You're not responsible for my happiness," said Celine.

"I know but I could have been a better friend."

"Where is your girlfriend? Celine said sarcastically. She secretly hoped he had dumped Nina.

"Nina and her sister are in the waiting room. They'd like to see you."

Celine gasped.

"I'm not ready to see them yet," she said. Even though she could not care less if she ever saw them again.

"Sure, I'll let them know that you're tired."

"Yes, I'm very tired." Celine yawned loudly.

Mando laughed. "I can take a hint. I'm glad to see you're recovering."

"Yeah. Sure."

Mando raised an eyebrow. "I mean it."

"Of course, you do, Mando. I'm just tired."

Celine turned her back to him, and Mando left the room quietly.

The next morning, Alex returned with beautiful flowers and convinced Celine to take his suite. Later that day, she went back to her bunk with her Bot to get her things and take them back to the Captain's hall where Alex and the highest paying guests slept.

Anna was sitting on her bunk and saw Celine removing her things.

"Where are you going?" she asked.

Celine didn't bother to answer, even though she liked Anna better than Nina. Celine had decided she didn't care to have either of the twins as her friends. They couldn't be a part of that tribe her father had said she would one day find.

She and her Valet Bot left the sleeping hall and didn't bother to look back.

When she arrived at the hall of suites, the concierge called Alex to show her the new sleeping quarters. Alex changed the code so the suite would accept her face image to unlock the door. When she stepped into the suite, she was amazed that it was so large and beautiful. *How could one person justify having so much space?* she thought.

"This is all for me?" she asked Alex.

"Yes, all 135 square meters."

"My word!"

Not even Admin at the Compound has this much living space.

The large room was divided into three sections. Celine's eyes landed on the circular sunken burnt orange couch that had a white marble table in the center. On the table was the latest hologram projector, Alex told her.

"Movies look very real, 4-D life-size."

She looked in amazement at what had to be the largest bed ever.

"King plus size," said Alex as he enjoyed watching Celine taking it all in.

"It's like a mini-apartment," he continued.

Hard to imagine why you would call it mini.

"This is all mine?" she asked. She was giddy.

"Yes," he said as he opened the door to a private bathroom.

"Well, I have to leave now," he said. "I have an appointment with the masseuse. Enjoy."

He paused at the doorway. "Oh, there's popcorn in the cabinet."

"What's popcorn," she yelled quickly.

"A snack. Just fine the bag and enjoy it."

As soon as he left, Celine flopped into the large bed with her Robo Pug and turned him on. It barked and its dark brown eyes lit up. As it wagged its short tail, it appeared to be enjoying itself as it licked her face with its scratchy tongue. It acted as if it had never been turned off. Celine giggled. She sat Puggie in her lap and rubbed his smooth, life-like fur.

"You're my friend, aren't you boy," she said as tears ran down her cheek, but these were happy tears. Her pug barked and licked her tears away.

Then suddenly, it jumped from her lap and ran to the edge of the bed. It began barking at something. When Celine glanced up to see what her dog was barking at, she saw a fruit fly walking on the ceiling.

"Ha-ha. Silly dog. It's just a little fly."

A second glance at it, made her wonder if it was real. It appeared to be emitting waves.

Then she was startled by an image of the concierge that emanated from a small globe next to the bed. When she glanced back at the ceiling, the fly was gone.

"Sorry to disturb you, Miss Red Cloud. You have a visitor, a Miss Venera Novik. Should I send her to your suite?" said the hologram.

"Oh yes, please do!"

When the doorbell rang, Celine could hardly contain herself.

"Open," she said excitedly.

The door slid open and Venera peeked in.

"Oh Celine, this suite is so beautiful! How are you?"

Celine smiled. "I'm fine. Come in."

Venera stepped into the suite and wrapped her arms around Celine, squeezing her tightly.

"I'm so glad you're safe and healthy and are staying in the best suites on the ship," she chuckled. "I'm surprised you know Alex Rittenhouse, the celebrity and son to one of the richest people on planet Earth. How did you meet him?"

"Last year, his father brought him to Mars."

"Whatever for?" Venera said as she sat on the sofa and gently pulled Celine next to her.

"To learn the family business, I think."

"Oh my! Small Universe."

Celine looked surprised by Venera's remark and then they both burst into laughter.

"I sometimes wonder, how big the Universe is and where is everyone?" said Venera.

"I'm worried about Alex though," said Celine. "He's changed. He used to be afraid of nothing. Now he's wearing camouflage suits and hiding from his dad."

"Young lady. You have enough problems of your own to worry about and to solve. Let Alex solve his own problems."

Celine agreed with Venera, but she had a tinge of guilt because she felt like it was her fault that Alex was no longer his adventurous fearless self. When her dad was lost in a dust storm last year, Alex had tried to help her find him and nearly lost his life.

Venera interrupted Celine's line of thinking.

"Have you thought about forgiving the twins?"

"Humph! Not really."

Celine didn't want to talk about the twins, they were a problem she was not ready to deal with. However, Venera seemed determined to talk about them so Celine listened.

"They've had a difficult childhood," said Venera. "They were born conjoined at the head and have experienced many surgeries, especially Nina."

Celine swallowed, then hardened her resolve.

"They lied about me, and now my parents and the Smiths think poorly of me."

"I know, and that's awful. But do you think you can forgive them?"

Celine exhaled. "Not yet. Maybe not ever."

Then her mentor asked her to put her left hand over her heart, her right hand over her left, and to repeat after her. Celine trusted Venera so she did as she was told.

"I want you to close your eyes and take a slow deep breath in and then exhale and continue taking these nice long breaths."

As Celine did, she began to lose the tension she hadn't realized she had been harboring.

"Think about compassion. Think about how that feels."

The reluctant teen did, and for a moment she felt compassion for Nina. It was such a surprise that she quickly opened her eyes and found her older friend smiling at her.

All those horrible things I had planned to do to the twins, that's not who I am. I am a loving person, and love and compassion feel so much better than hate.

She looked around at her beautiful suite and thought how grateful she was that Alex had given her such a beautiful place to stay. Then she took in the face of her caring friend.

"Thank you for that experience. Thank you for checking on me."

Her friend smiled warmly.

"Looks like you're doing just fine," she said. "And please think about what I said about forgiveness. It could keep you from being a victim twice."

Celine didn't answer. She had said all that she wanted to say about the twins.

As soon as Venera left Celine opened her flute case, pulled out her flute, and began to play a song that suddenly came to her. Her dad had taught her how to play by ear, to listen to music and to play what she heard, and she could hear F#, C# and A#. She played the notes over and over and it lifted her spirits. She closed her eyes and smiled. The fly had returned to the ceiling and sat motionless, but made a soft buzzing sound that mimicked the music Celine had just played.

CHAPTER 14

EUROPA

The next day, Alex came over to see how Celine was enjoying the suite.

"Love it. More than I could have ever imagined," she said.

Alex's eyes lit up and a broad smile beamed across his face.

"You deserve it," he said.

Celine blushed and she quickly changed the subject.

"What happened with the astronauts who landed on Europa? Did I sleep through all the excitement?"

"You didn't miss much. The only thing they've found was an icy, watery wasteland."

"No land to build a settlement?" she asked with disappointment.

Alex shook his head no.

"Maybe a Brandenberg refueling platform could be set up one day, but it'll probably be manned by roBots. I can't imagine anyone wanting to live on a platform above icy water."

"What a disappointment. I was hoping Europa would become an outback settlement. I guess Mars will have to keep that title for a little longer," she sighed.

Alex chuckled.

"So, I didn't come over here to talk to you about Europa. This evening, I am having a party in my suite, and you're invited."

"Oh? But your birthday isn't for another month."

"I'm not having a birthday party," Alex laughed. "I'm having a movie party!"

Celine raised an eyebrow. Unlike the Mars' colonists, *Earth's people have so many parties.*

"I'll have the latest action movie, *Real Cowboys!* We'll have old-fashioned junk food, like hotdogs, fries, and fruit punch."

"Yuk. People on Earth used to eat dogs?"

Puggie, who had been lying on the bed, began to whine.

"Don't worry, pooch. No one would ever eat you," Alex laughed. "So, are you coming to my party?" he asked Celine.

"Sure. I really want to see *Real Cowboys*, but I might pass on the old-fashioned junk food. So don't fix any for me."

"I'll let you smell the food first. I think you'll change your mind. One other thing, there's a fashion printer in the closet.

Why don't you check out the latest fashions. Print any outfit you want. You can keep it if you like or throw it back into the printer storage bin to be recycled after you've worn it."

Celine beamed. *Am I dreaming? Alex, the best-looking boy on Earth, has just invited me to his party and is giving me an outfit to wear to it.*

"Thank you," she said softly. She knew that on Mars, a fashion printer would have been seen as an unnecessary use of energy. She was almost embarrassed to receive such a gift. What would her parents think of such waste?

"You deserve it," he said. "I wish I had told you I was coming to Mars or at least that I was on The Fantasy. I'm sorry that I didn't tell you."

Celine had never heard Alex apologize for anything. She was flabbergasted.

"You've changed," she said.

"Yes, I have." Alex sat on the gold sofa and motioned Celine to sit next to him. "I've been working part-time with my dad."

"What? Your dad?"

"Yeah! Learning the family business."

"I thought you didn't like the family business."

Alex sucked his teeth.

"What about your Media Show? You haven't made any since you left Mars. Why not?"

Alex stood up and began heading towards the door.

"I thought you would be more understanding. You know that my dad wants me to work in the business. It's the best thing for me."

"No! That's not true. Those caves in the red hills ruined you and it's all my fault."

Celine's eyes teared up.

"It's not your fault. Sure, I wanted to help you find your dad, but that wasn't the only reason I went to the Chaos Region with you."

"Oh? I know that I put us in a lot of danger last year. We shouldn't have been out there looking for my dad. Mars is too dangerous. Too unpredictable. I could have gotten us killed."

"I had my own reasons for going out there. I thought your dad had the coordinates for the ores."

"Coordinates?"

"Yes. I wanted to get my hands on those coordinates before my father did—maybe he would have thought I was worthy..." Alex said as he lowered his eyebrows.

"I don't understand." *How could a Media Star like Alex feel unworthy?*

"It's okay. I made the decision to go. You gave me the opportunity. Nothing was your fault. Okay?"

"Okay," Celine said reluctantly. "Will you ever do your adventure shows again?"

"I don't know. The Martian caves have given me reasons to be more cautious."

After Alex left, Celine went straight to the closet to see the fashion printer. There were so many outfits in this printer's database, she hardly knew where to start. She decided to search the data by color and quickly found a red jumpsuit that reminded her of the red dust on Mars. She typed her size into the printer, and in a matter of minutes the outfit was ready to wear. The red jumpsuit was highlighted with sparkly silver threads, and it fitted her lean figure as if it had been painted on. She unbraided her hair and brushed it loose. Then looked in the long mirror on the bathroom wall. *I look beautiful.* Celine gasped. *Did I just say that?* She had never thought of herself as beautiful, but today she did, and she hoped that Alex would think she was beautiful too.

Promptly at eighteen hundred hours, she went over to Alex's suite. Mr. Abiola let her in.

The suite was exactly like hers. She entered the room confidently, holding her head high, stepping lightly, almost gliding across the floor as she had seen the twins do. Then she sat on the edge of the circular couch and crossed her legs.

Mr. Abiola cleared his throat. "Alex will be out shortly," he said as he nodded toward the bathroom.

"Would you like anything? Fruit punch? Water?"

"Water would be fine," she said. "The water on this ship is delicious."

Mr. Abiola nodded. "If you say so. It must be those fabulously expensive water filters."

He ran a glass of water from the refrigerator door and handed it to her. Then the doorbell buzzed. When the door slid open, Mando and the twins walked in. Fortunately for Celine, Alex stepped out of the bathroom just as she was considering leaving the suite. He was dressed in a pair of shorts bejeweled with three taser jewels and a plain white shirt and he looked so cute.

"Oh, Celine, you look beautiful," he said when he saw her.

It was exactly what she had hoped to hear. She slid back in her seat.

Then Alex noticed Mando and the twins, waiting near the doorway.

"Hi, Mando. Hello, ladies."

"Hey, Alex. I hope you don't mind that I brought my girlfriend and her sister with me. They haven't seen the movie and were dying to see it."

Celine noticed Nina elbow Mando.

"This is Nina," he said as if mesmerized by her. "And Anna her sister."

Each girl put the palms of their hands together and nodded their heads when Mando said their names.

Celine didn't miss the smirk on Nina's face as they entered the suite.

"I thought your trip to Mars was a secret," Celine said to Alex.

"I couldn't have a movie party without inviting Mando to the party. Besides, I have him to thank for recording your show."

"What about your dad?"

"I'm sure he knows I'm here by now, but we're only two weeks away from the moon so he won't be too angry now that we're close to home."

"I wish I could say the same," Celine mumbled.

"I love your new style," said Anna who, like her sister, was dressed in a plain pink jumpsuit.

"Thanks," Celine said flatly.

"I'm so excited to see the newest movies," said Nina. "I wanted to see them when we were on Mars, but we were only getting..."

"I know, the older movies," Celine said with a smirk.

"You look beautiful," said Mando. "I've never seen you look so lovely."

Nina gave him another elbow to his side.

He chuckled and said, "No one is more beautiful than you, Nina."

Nina smirked at Celine.

Anna said, "But I'm her twin."

Alex laughed, but Mando's face showed not a hint of laughter at Anna's comment.

Celine didn't even bother to smile with closed lips but rolled her eyes at the two girls she once adored.

"This is going to be an interesting party," said Mr. Abiola. "I've seen the movie so I'm going to the gym for a workout. Is everything okay?" He directed his question to Alex.

"I hope so. See you in three hours."

Mr. Abiola opened the door to leave, and a chef rolled in a cart full of hot foods for the party. As he did, a small black fly flew past him and into the party suite without notice.

It lit on the wall near the ceiling, close to the circular couch.

The scent of the hot food, especially the scent of hot buttered popcorn, had everyone eager to eat.

"There are burgers, hotdogs, fries, popcorn, and red fruit punch!" said Alex eagerly, and beckoned everyone to serve themselves.

Everyone but Anna, who had left for the bathroom, piled their plates high. Then found a space on the couch in front of the hologram projector. The fly flew down from the ceiling to the table near the plates of food. Its abdomen lit up like a firefly's. Suddenly the four teens were enveloped in what appeared to be a glass bubble, vanishing just as Anna stepped out of the bathroom. She screamed and ran into the hall.

"Somebody, help! My sister disappeared!"

Then the fly flew past her and headed into the flower garden, next to the Smiths' suite.

The Smiths and the Ballingers were having dinner together. They were seated on the circular couch, like the ones that were in all the guest suites, gold-colored smooth velvet cushions with high backs. Their Valet Bots were serving them coffee.

"This coffee is the best in the universe," said Mrs. Smith as she lifted her cup, making certain the Ballingers could see a very large diamond on her ring finger. She took a sip from her gold-trimmed coffee cup.

"The coffee beans were raised on the Moon in low gravity. I think that's what gives it such a unique flavor."

Mrs. Ballinger took a sip from her cup and then stifled a cough.

"Extravagant," she said with a faked smile.

Then the buzzer to the Smiths' suite rang interrupting the wives' bogus chat.

"Come on in," yelled Mr. Smith.

Two hefty chefs dressed in white suits entered the suite pushing two carts of steaming hot food.

"Leave the carts next to the door," said Mr. Smith and he slipped a tip card into each of their waiting hands. As they opened the door to leave, the tiny fly flew past them unnoticed. It flew to the ceiling right above the circular couch.

Mr. Smith and Mr. Ballinger removed the dishes from the carts, loaded them with food, and then placed them on the round white marble table. As soon as the two men were seated with their wives, the fly flew down and landed on the table. Then its abdomen lit up like a firefly. Mr. Smith noticed it right away. He quickly pulled off a shoe and began hammering the fly with it. A loud popping sound came from the fly and then the light on its abdomen went out and tiny metal legs flew from it in all directions. Mrs. Smith looked appalled.

"What are you doing?" she screamed.

"The teens are up to their same tricks," Mr. Smith said as he lifted the damaged fly parts from the table and floor. I saw Celine making this in the media room."

"Oh, disgusting," Mrs. Smith said as she got up and ran to the restroom in tears.

"Now they've done it!" said Mr. Smith. "Dr. Vee will have to do something about those teens." His fist tensed. "You folks," he said to the Ballingers. "You stay. Enjoy your brisket, but I've got business to tend to."

"Why don't we join you another time," said Mr. Ballinger. "We can try the brisket when we can all eat together. We'll see you later."

As the Ballingers were leaving, Mr. Smith stomped out of his suite, heading to the administration office, making an awkward sound as he walked quickly down the hall in one shoe. In his haste, he had one shoe in his hand and the damaged insect in the other. When he entered the administrative complex, he was surprised to see several military personnel.

"What's going on?" he asked.

"Security checks," lied Dr. Vee, not wanting the other guests to know of the teens' disappearance and the military presence. "How may I help you, Mr. Smith?"

Dr. Vee's nose was red, and his eyes were watery as if he had been crying, a very peculiar sight for the director who was always happy. However, Mr. Smith was too angry to notice.

"It's those teens," he shouted. "They put this spy thing in my suite."

He handed the mechanical fly to Dr. Vee.

"So sorry, sir. I'll take care of this."

"Yes! Do something or you'll be looking for another job next year," spat Mr. Smith as he left the room.

Dr. Vee handed the metallic fly to his assistant.

"Add this to the printer scraps," he said.

"What's this?" said the assistant. "This is metal. Our printers don't get hot enough to make anything out of metal."

One of the Space Force Cadets overheard the assistant.

"Let me see it," he said.

The assistant handed the metal over to the cadet, whose eyes lit up as he studied the mechanical fly.

"Lieutenant, I think we might have something here. This thing is not made of any metal that I'm familiar with," he said.

Celine remembered a glass-like bubble surrounding her. Except for the loud scream from Anna, she felt detached from her surroundings. She felt cold and couldn't move. Then she saw an image of herself as if she was looking in a life-size mirror. She continued to watch the image as she felt a tingling sensation moved from her head to her toes. It didn't hurt but it felt like the gravity machine had been turned off. She knew she was moving toward something, but she had no way to stop it. She began to tremble as if every cell in her body was vibrating at a higher-than-normal frequency. She continued to watch the image of herself, and she noticed that it was dissolving into a puddle of dirty water. As it did, Celine felt as she had been splashed by a warm shower. Then in a flash, the puddle turned into a cloud of dust and Celine felt like she was floating. The dust cloud appeared to be following her. She continued to watch the dust float through dark space and seep through an asteroid as if it were a hologram then floated into an enclosure. The dust floated toward her, and Celine suddenly realized that this dust cloud was her physical form broken down into its minerals. She was merely consciousness floating through space. A wave of panic ran over her. *Am I dead? Am I a spirit?* She wanted to cry, to scream! *I didn't get a chance to say goodbye to my family.* But she could only think it. Not say it.

Then she began to feel the same tingling sensation she felt when the bubble first surrounded her. For a moment she felt as if she was in two places at the same time, in the Fantasy

Spaceship, and in a strange new room. She looked down to see her hands and legs materializing. She shivered, wrapped her arms around her chest, and then toppled over onto a dirt floor.

Later that day Anna was called in to speak with Lieutenant Adeyemi of Earth Space Force. He questioned her about what happened, but he was also very interested that she and Nina were identical twins and had been joined at the head. This thing was extremely rare, but only happened to babies who were conceived and born in low gravity. Their mother must have spent a lot of time in deep space.

"Can you communicate with each other from a distance?" the lieutenant asked Anna.

"Yes."

His eyes lit up, and he nodded and smiled with new purpose.

"Have you ever had the same thoughts?" he continued.

"Oh no, we're very different," said Anna, who wanted to help find her sister.

"What I'm asking is can the two of you communicate with telepathy?"

"No. I don't think so."

"Well, how do you communicate with each other from a distance?"

"My sister has a BCI."

"A Brain-Computer Interface?"

"Yes."

"So, you can send her computer messages directly to her implant."

"Yes."

"Breakthrough!" said the lieutenant as he leaned back in his chair. "Thank you, Anna. You've been very helpful. You may leave now."

"Sir, I think we're going to need her," said a cadet.

"Wait a minute, Anna. We're going to need your help. We need you to contact your sister."

Dr. Vee was so upset that the children were missing. He had the entire ship, inside and outside, searched several times. *How will I tell the parents their children are missing, and we have no idea where they are?*

He and Mr. Abiola weren't permitted into Alex's suite since the Space Force took over.

They had both searched the suite earlier for clues and had come up empty-handed, and what Anna said made no sense to Mr. Abiola. But Dr. Vee thought the teens might have been kidnapped by the Old Guardians.

His parents had told him and his siblings stories of a strange race of beings who took young couples to seed other worlds. They thought it as their spiritual mandate to seed the universe with humankind. These beings had been to his planet several times and kidnapped couples. It was told in the folklore that once they had taken someone, you never saw them again. Dr. Vee sighed.

CHAPTER 15

THE ASTEROID

Celine awoke, lying on a dirt floor. Her head throbbed and she felt light-headed. Carefully, she sat up. Her eyes took in everything; having lived on Mars had taught her to be very aware of her surroundings. She noticed that three walls of the room were made of gray-colored rock and the fourth was dark and shiny, almost glass-like, making it nearly impossible to tell if someone was watching her. There was a small fountain of running water in a corner. Next to the fountain was a trough of an unfamiliar green vegetable. She could see steam rising above it and it had an unfamiliar scent but not unpleasant. In the opposite corner was a small stone platform with a spigot half a meter above it, and it appeared to have a circular- shaped hole in its floor. She had never seen anything like it, but then she had never seen a bathtub until she stayed on The Fantasy.

She saw Mando and Nina lying next to each other on the dirt floor. She couldn't tell if they were dead or alive. To the left of her, and lying motionless with his face in the dirt, was Alex.

She whispered his name. He lifted a finger and opened an eye and then closed it. Still feeling a bit shaky, she crawled over to him and gently shook his shoulder.

"Wake up, Alex," she pleaded. "Please, wake up."

His breathing became deeper, and he tried to brush her hand away. Finally,

he turned over on his back and stared up at the cave-like ceiling.

"Not again," he said, referring to the time he had spent lost in a cave on Mars.

"I don't know where we are, but we're not on Mars. Look!" she whispered.

She pointed to the liquid which appeared to be water.

"I think we've been kidnapped by pirates."

Alex's eyes landed on the water and food as he sat up and brushed the dirt from the side of his face.

"What the heck is going on? That's an animal trough. Is this some kind of joke?"

"I don't think so. There's Mando and Nina."

Celine looked in their direction. She noticed Mando and Nina were quietly sitting up. Mando was helping Nina reposition her lavender wig on her head. Celine was surprised to see that a part of Nina's head shone like polished metal. She leaned in a little closer to get a better look.

What happened to Nina?

When Nina noticed Celine looking at her, she rolled her eyes and quickly patted her wig in place. Celine politely turned away, but not before noticing Mando kissing Nina on the forehead.

"What happened?" Nina asked. "Where are we?"

"We're trying to figure that out," said Alex. He had already gotten up and walked the perimeter of the room, looking for a way out.

Nina slipped an arm under Mando's, as if he could protect her.

"There are no doors in here," Alex said as he studied the glass-like wall. "I wonder why such a small room would have such tall ceilings."

He turned toward Celine. "What do you see, Martian Girl?"

"Who put you in charge?" Nina chimed in.

Alex ignored her.

Celine stood up and studied the glass wall that extended from the dirt floor to its four-meter-high ceiling. In the lower-left corner of the glass wall, she noticed a tall door-sized portion that seemed to be distorted light. She walked toward it and hesitantly touched it.

Buzz!

"Ouch!"

Celine stumbled back.

"This must be the door, but I think it's…"

"Well, what are we waiting for? Let's get out of here," said Nina as she jumped up and ran into the full force of the invisible door.

"Wait," said Celine. But it was too late.

Nina was knocked off her feet and landed on her back in the dirt. For a moment she lay there as if she was in shock, staring at the ceiling. Then she snapped back to life and gave out a howl that reminded Celine of a wild dog.

"My goodness," said Mando. "What have you done?"

He ran to Nina and cautiously touched her. Then he took her into his arms and began to rock her back and forth.

"Don't just stand there. Get some help!" He yelled at Alex.

Celine advanced toward the barrier.

"Hey, don't do that," said Alex. "You don't want to end up like her," he chuckled, trying hard not to laugh at the girl who had caused Celine so much grief.

"There's someone there," said Celine.

She sucked in air and stepped back.

"Let us out of here!" yelled Mando.

"What did you see?" asked Alex. The hair on his arms was raised. "Your eyes can see things that normal eyes can't," he said for the benefit of Nina and Mando who did not know of Celine's gifted eyes.

She turned her head just enough to look at Alex, but she did not take her eyes off the glass wall.

"I don't know—but it's very tall and it's glowing white like a light."

"What? I don't see anything," said Mando who was still on the dirt floor with Nina in his arms.

"I don't either, but trust me, if Celine sees something, it's there," said Alex. "Let's move back here," he said as he nodded toward the back of the room, realizing the room had no place to hide. Everyone proceeded to the rear as instructed.

"It's gone," Celine said as she wrapped her arms around her chest, her heart racing as if she was back in the water-filled space suit.

Nina, though still wobbly from the powerful energy shock, lifted her pointed chin, and stared over her straight nose at Celine.

"I don't see anything special about her," she mumbled.

As Celine stared back at Nina, she wondered how she could ever have wanted to be like her.

Now that I'm seeing the real you, I don't see anything special about you either. Your behavior is so ugly, it steals your beauty, so you're not beautiful to me anymore. You're a mean girl and I don't like you.

Instead of sharing her true feelings, she said, "Are you okay?"

"Do you really care?" Nina asked as she put her hands on her hips.

Celine thought about the question for a moment. Yes, she cared. Even though she didn't like Nina anymore, she didn't want her to get hurt.

"Stop it!" said Alex.

Both girls raised their eyebrows and slowly turned their heads in his direction. Alex ran his fingers through his hair, then opened his eyes wide as he stepped back from them.

"Can you really see things that normal people can't see?" asked Mando.

The question left Celine speechless. Hearing him use the words 'normal people' made her heart sink.

"I guess I'm not normal," she replied sadly.

Alex spoke up for her. "Being normal is overrated. Celine is gifted and her gift might be the thing we need to get us out of this mess."

"Ha!" said Mando. "Your dad's money is the thing that will get us out of this mess."

"What do you mean?" asked Alex as he stabbed his finger at Mando.

Mando flinched but continued speaking.

"Everyone knows your dad has billions of credits."

"Yeah, what of it?" Alex said as his right hand slid down to one of the taser jewels on his pants.

Celine noticed. She remembered how the taser had stopped her Puggie and that the doctor called the jewels, rich kids' weapons.

"Guys," she said. "We don't know if pirates have kidnapped us. What I saw might not be human."

Both boys faced her and even Nina seemed interested.

"I saw a tall being, much taller than any male I've seen."

"Well, that doesn't mean anything. You haven't seen much living on that outback planet," said Nina.

"What did you see?" asked Alex and Mando in unison.

Staring into space as if she couldn't find the right words to describe the disturbing sight, she finally answered.

"It was like a tall being made of bright light."

"Could that be a tall person in camouflage?" asked Alex.

"Does Earth have people who are three meters tall?"

"Three meters! That's ten feet!' Yelled Mando. "Of course not!"

Celine continued. "I've never seen a bright white aura around a person. And there was a strange scent coming from it that reminded me of the Meat Lab. Didn't you smell it?"

"I don't know. Everything in here smells," Alex said as he looked at Mando.

Mando smirked but didn't reply.

"How would I know what a meat lab smells like? I wouldn't be caught dead in one," smirked Nina.

"Look, I know you ladies don't care much for each other, but this is the wrong time for conflict among us," said Alex as stared at Nina.

Celine shook her head. "I know."

"You and Mando need to stop it too," said Nina.

Alex exhaled loudly, "You're right. We all need to put our conflicts aside."

"I have no problems with Celine," said Mando. "I think we're still friends." He tilted his head and smiled at Celine.

"Nina?" asked Alex. "Can you and Celine settle your differences?" He looked around at the tiny cave-like room. "Another place? Another time?" he added.

"Of course," said her mouth, but her words did not reach her eyes.

"We need a plan to get out of here," he continued. "And we'll have to work together. Understood?"

Mando nodded. And so did Nina after some nudging from Mando.

"I agree," said Celine. She was glad to see Alex was taking charge.

Then Alex turned to her. "What's the plan?"

Meanwhile, on the Fantasy, twelve Space Warriors from the Earth Space Force team had arrived to help solve the problem.

They arrived on their newest and fastest ship. Shaped like a black triangle. It was two-hundred square meters in size, a lot smaller than the luxury Fantasy ship, but extremely powerful. The ship could create its own wormhole to jump enormous distances through space. Only the military owned such a powerful ship. They arrived from the military base on Earth's moon in only one day. It would take The Fantasy two weeks to travel that distance.

Two of their engineers had quickly reverse-engineered the mechanical fly. They knew the signal to the fly had come from the asteroid, and Nina's CBI locator's signal was also on that asteroid.

That asteroid, or one like it, had been seen in the Virgo Supercluster three years ago. Its cylinder-shaped appearance and unnatural movements had raised questions among members of Earth and Mars Military Space Forces. At the time, the military didn't have a spacecraft fast enough to reach the strange asteroid before it entered the Asteroid Belt and disappeared as it passed Ceres. However, thanks to Mr. Rittenhouse, Alex's dad and the founder of the Martian colony, Earth's military forces now had such a ship. They hope they would find technologies that could be added to their ever-growing arsenals. Their only concern was they didn't know the ship's defense capabilities.

They considered themselves lucky to have a bionic like Nina on board the asteroid. It was like dropping a secret spy on an enemy ship. She could record the interior of the ship and maybe even download all its files.

"And if we can't board it before it enters the asteroid belt, we could use the Particle Disruptor on it and collect the pieces."

"What about the teens?" asked Dr. Vee, who had been waiting to hear the rescue plans.

The Space Warrior was surprised that Dr. Vee was in the room.

"Sir, you'll have to leave," he said.

Two of the warriors headed toward Dr. Vee to remove him from the room.

"Getting those young people safely back on this ship is imperative!" he said.

"Remove him," said the Space Warrior lieutenant. "Getting that data from that asteroid is imperative!"

"We'll see about that," Dr. Vee said as he twirled his colorful coat around and exited the room.

"Sir, what about the teens?" asked the concerned second lieutenant of the captain.

"I guess they'll have to keep their heads down," said the captain. "You think those teens know how to keep their heads down?"

"Yes sir," responded all the Space Warriors with military discipline.

Meanwhile, Dr. Vee walked quickly, almost running down the hall to Mr. Abiola's suite. When Mr. Abiola opened the door, Dr. Vee almost fell into his arms. Holding his hand over the right side of his chest above his two pounding hearts, he took a long deep breath. He looked up at the concerned face of Mr. Abiola.

"We have to get in touch with Alex's dad," he said in one breath.

∾

Back on the asteroid…

"They're treating us just like animals," complained Nina. "Do they not know that I come from a long line of important Samurai?"

She stared indignantly at Alex.

"And you're a superstar. Doesn't that count for something?"

Alex looked at Nina in disbelief. "Amazing," he said as he shook his head. "Can't you see that whoever has taken us doesn't care about those things? Do you see that hole in the floor?"

"Yes, but why does that matter?" Nina said with a confused look on her frustrated face.

"That's our toilet, Miss Princess. One hole in the floor for the four of us!"

Nina gasped and lifted her hand to her throat, as if suppressing her urge to throw up.

Mando said, "This is all your fault that we've been kidnapped. Someone wants some of your dad's wealth. They really want you, not us. We don't have any."

"Mando, that's not fair," said Celine. "Remember your promise. We don't know where we are or who has us."

Mando seemed to get more frustrated as he watched Alex pick up a vegetable that looked like a baked green potato, peeled the skin back, and took a bite.

"What are you doing?" Mando asked weakly.

Like the other teens, he was hungry and dehydrated but determined to not feed or drink like an animal from a trough.

"I'm hungry, "Alex said. "We haven't had food or water in two days! We have no idea how to get out of here. When the opportunity occurs, I want to be strong enough to …follow Celine's plan."

"How do you know it's not poisoned?" whispered Nina.

"If they didn't want us alive, we wouldn't be having this conversation. Besides, don't they want my dad's credits? If that's the case, they'd want us to stay alive."

Mando looked at Alex in disgust. Celine noticed the expression on Mando's face and wondered if he was jealous of Alex. After all, she had certainly bragged about him.

"Here, eat some," said Alex.

He broke off a piece of the vegetable and tried to hand it to Mando, who pushed Alex's hand aside abruptly. Alex laughed and offered the food to Nina, who quickly stepped back and wrinkled her nose.

"I'm hungry, too, but I've never eaten green potatoes from an animals' trough. And I don't plan to start now," said Mando. "Help yourself."

"Me neither," said Nina as she folded her strong arms in front of her flat chest. "And I'm not lapping water from a fountain," she continued. "I'd rather die first."

"Suit yourself," said Alex. "We've been here two days. You could die in three days without water and a few weeks without food. I plan to live."

"Don't talk about death. Whoever or whatever has taken us doesn't want us to die," said Celine. "I think the water and food are safe."

She cupped her hands, scooped up some water, and lapped it up.

"It tastes good," she said as she scooped up another handful of water. She had not seen the Being of light since they arrived. She wondered if they would ever get the opportunity to escape the dinky room.

"I want to get out of here," said Nina.

"We all do," said Celine. "But we'll all have a clearer head once we have had food and water."

As Mando was about to get a drink of water, one of Nina's eye lit up.

"Wait, I hear something. It's Anna. I have a message from my sister."

Her eyes opened wider as she listened. "She's sent me a voice message."

"She has a Brain-Computer Implant," said Mando proudly when he saw the confusion on Celine's face.

So that explains the shiny head.

"What did she say?" Celine asked Nina.

"She said don't worry. She said she's on Earth's Space Force Ship with the Space Warriors not far from us. She said the warriors are working on a plan to rescue us."

"They are? That's wonderful!"

"Wait a minute. Let me replay this." Nina's right eye lit up as she listened to the message a second time.

"That can't be right," Nina said in a choking voice. "Why do all the bad things happen to me?"

"What do you mean?" asked Mando in a caring voice.

Nina swallowed. "Anna said…" We're on an alien spaceship heading toward the Asteroid Belt."

"You mean like an ET spaceship?" asked Mando.

Nina nodded her head yes, stared at the ceiling, then continued. "They believe that when will reach the Asteroid Belt, we will vanish as we pass Ceres. She said we have two days."

Later that night, when the lights were down low to mimic night, Celine couldn't fall asleep. She rested her head on her arms, trying to keep her hair off the dirt floor.

She replayed Anna's message in her head.

We're on an alien ship, on our way to the Asteroid Belt. We'll be further from Earth than Mars.

Even if the Warriors could save them, she didn't think they could get her back to Earth in time to meet her grandma. Tears rolled down her cheek as she sobbed quietly and stared at the glass wall that imprisoned her. Then she heard something moving outside her cage. She let her hair fall across her face, hiding her eyes as she peeked through the curls. She watched as the energized door disappeared and a tall being entered. Though the room was dimly lit, she could see its ashen armored-like skin, or was it a jumpsuit? It was hard to tell. A tiny cart was wheeled in behind the giant and Celine watched in revulsion as it used its uncovered six-fingered hands to lift and gently place more green potatoes in the trough.

She gasped. It turned to look in her direction. She quickly closed her eyes. When she reopened them, the alien appeared to be testing the water. She could hear it humming a tune that sounded more like growling a tune. When the Being finished its tasks, she noticed that it stood near the doorway for a moment as if it was waiting for the energized door to reopen. Celine watched closely as a round disk on the floor blinked twice. The doorway cleared, and the giant stepped out, slowly dragging the cart full of potatoes behind it.

CHAPTER 16

WE DON'T BELONG HERE

On the Space Warriors ship, Captain Orlov dictated the codes for the app that Nina would need to download everything she saw on the asteroid ship. He incorporated the math and the strange musical notes the engineers had gotten from the mechanical fly. He and his team wanted the data so badly they were willing to do anything to get it. He knew that he would be putting the teens in more danger, and that it might be easier to simply focus on their rescue, but with Nina Emoto, a bionic, on the alien ship, he would not pass up the opportunity to exploit it.

He hoped the data would help him and his team take over this alien ship. He did not know if it posed a danger to Earth. He didn't care if it came in peace. His only care was about the data he would get. As a warrior, he needed to be exceptional in all things. Suddenly he was interrupted by a call from his superior from Earth.

"Yes ma'am, General ma'am. We appreciate the ship Mr. Rittenhouse practically gave us. Yes, ma'am. Understood. Over and out."

Captain Orlov took a deep breath. He was not happy that his plans had been given to his superiors. After all, having this data could bring about the technology needed to keep Earth's Space Force superior to all possible threats. He had every intention of rescuing the teens. Now, he would have to tell his fellow space warriors that their mission had changed. Getting the alien data would no longer be their primary mission. Their primary mission was now a rescue mission.

"I guess this is not a normal kidnapping after all," said Mando.

"We're on an asteroid heading away from Earth," stuttered Celine. "I won't be meeting my grandmother in two weeks. In fact, I might not ever see my family again. Never see my baby brother." Her cheeks and nose turned red, and her eyes teared up.

"How do we get out of this situation? Nina? When is Anna going to contact you again?" said Mando. "I'm beginning to feel claustrophobic. This room feels like it's closing in on me."

"Let's everyone stay calm," whispered Alex. He looked toward the window and decided to turn his back to it before speaking. "Celine said she watched a giant come in here last night to replenish our rations. Tell them what you saw, Celine."

Celine described the giant and told them about the blinking disk on the floor.

"I took a look at it, and it looks pretty simple," said Alex. "If I can short that disk with one of my tasers, I can get us out of here."

"Then what?" asked Mando. "We're on an ET ship! What's outside this room? We don't even know if there's oxygen out there."

"I'm willing to take a chance. We must find a way to take over this ship."

"What about Celine's plan?"

"We'll use it when we have to," said Celine. "But for now, we need to learn more about this ship."

Suddenly Celine looked up at the doorway. The light Being had entered the room.

"It's here," she said as she watched the tall figure of light stand in front of the food bin as if checking the food allocation.

She and Alex had eaten one each of the green potatoes. Nina and Mando had eaten nothing. She watched the light Being move toward a panel located above the water fountain. The being stayed there as if reading the symbols. Then it turned quickly as if it felt it was being watched. Celine immediately looked down. The other teens took their clue from her and looked down, picking at their fingernails or nervously rubbing their hands together. The Being returned its attention to the panel and then put its foot over the blinking disk on the floor near the energized door and left.

"It's gone," said Celine. "I don't think it realizes I can see it. I think the white light is some kind of camouflage."

"Why do you think that?" asked Mando.

"The light being and the giant that was in here while you slept, is the same size and they both have six fingers."

"Dang. Sorry I asked," said Mando as he pursed his lips.

Nina held up a finger to get everyone's attention.

"I have another message from Anna," Nina said with hope in her voice.

Everyone gathered around Nina, desperately wanting to know when the Space Force would come to save them.

"When are they coming?" asked Celine.

"I don't know," was Nina's reply. "They're close by, but they want us to do whatever we can to slow the ship down." She paused for a moment as if confused. "And they want me to take photos."

"Pictures?" Alex sounded angry. "Why?"

"How are we supposed to slow the ship down?" groaned Mando. "Do they realize we're trapped in a cage?"

"It doesn't matter," said Alex. "If we can't slow this ship, it looks like we're on our own."

Alex removed one of his taser jewels from his pants and held it up.

"This might be our way out of here," he said. "It has an electric charge. Maybe it could overload that thing on the floor, and the door will open."

He walked over to the small panel on the floor. Everyone quickly joined him.

"I saw the giant step on this before leaving," Celine said as she pointed to the round panel of the floor. She stepped on it, but nothing happened.

"What are you going to do with that taser?" asked Mando. "Fry yourself?"

Alex paused, then seemed to have second thoughts. He took off one of his shoes and placed it on the floor next to the taser. Then he used his shoe to push the taser to the panel. Just as the taser touched the panel, a spark flew from it and the taser flew up, hit the wall behind them, then fell into the water with a sizzle.

"Wow!" said Alex. His face had lost all color.

"Now what?" asked Mando.

Celine stood up and looked where the energized door had been.

"Alex, I think you did it. The door is gone."

Back on the Warrior's spaceship, the engineers were working on an app that they could send to Nina's implant to dampen her interface with their supercomputer. Supercomputers had been known to damage BCI implants. The signals from them are so strong they could cause the implants to go into extreme vibrations, causing them to crack. And with no medical help on the alien spaceship, this could be dangerous for Nina. If her implant cracked, she might not ever recover.

If Nina was willing to interface with the supercomputer, the engineers would send her the dampening app and the signals that would bounce off the walls of the alien ship creating a map of the ship's interior. Once they had that map, they would land on the asteroid, and find a way in to rescue the teens.

"I'm going out first," said Celine. "If any of the giants are in camouflage, I can see them."

"I'm right behind you," said Alex as he inhaled deeply. "Ah! Fresh air."

Mando and Nina followed. They all stood in front of their cage in total shock. They were in a hall of what appeared to be hundreds of cages like the one they had just left. Each appeared to contain human-like beings. Even from a distance, they could see that the beings were not exactly human. Some were blue in color, some had tiny slits where noses should be.

"Do you think they can see us?" asked Nina.

"I hope not," said Celine as she noticed that some of the caged humans had long pointed teeth.

"Which way do we go?" asked Mando.

Celine scanned the hall.

"It appears to be lighter at that end," she said and pointed past a row of cages.

"We could get lost in this place," said Mando.

He rushed back to the glass cage and grabbed two of the potatoes.

"So, you decided you're hungry now?" asked Alex in frustration.

"Yes, I am. But that's not why I got the potatoes. I'm going to mash a small piece on a wall whenever we make a turn. That way, we know how to get back."

"I can help with that," said Nina, who then went back into the room and returned with two potatoes. "One to smash and one to eat," she said.

"Amazing," said Alex with a smirk.

Celine led the way. In the first cage, the one next to theirs were four people: two girls and two boys. They looked just like ordinary teens but were a rich blue color. However, they wore blue clothes which could have easily been the reason their skin appeared blue. There were other young people in the cages, but there was always something about them that didn't seem quite human, like unusually large ears or eyes big and round, more like a frog than a human. As the teens passed the cages none of the people seemed aware of them.

Once they reached the end of the hall, they came upon a botanical garden of plants that not even Mando, whose parents were botanists, recognized. The room was well lit, but Celine wasn't sure of its source. She didn't see anything in the room that could help them take over a spaceship. Not unless these plants could run the ship.

"Well, now we know why you saw so much light down here," said Alex.

"Watch out," yelled Mando as he gave Celine a hard shove.

As she stumbled back, she noticed that one of the limbs of a plant was slithering away. The plant hissed like a snake as it returned to its trunk. Then a tiny yellow bird flew into the garden. Celine noticed right away that it did not have an aura.

"It's beautiful," said Nina.

"It's not real," said Celine as she looked around the garden for any signs of an entrance to another hall. "This is a dead-end," she said. "The Command Center must be at the other end of the hall."

As they left the atrium, all the lights went out. Nina stifled a scream.

"Celine, can you get us back to our home away from home," said Alex. "I don't think it's safe out here."

Celine studied the cages down the hall.

"I can see the auras of most of the people in the cages, but I'm not sure where to turn."

"I can help." said Mando. "I remember where I put the mashed potato. What about you, Nina?"

"You were doing such a good job, I ate both of mine," Nina replied,

Alex chuckled.

"Let's go now," said Celine. "I can see the aura of a very large spider."

"How large?" teased Alex.

"About the size of a large puppy," Celine shouted as she ran down the hall.

"Wait for me," screamed Alex.

When they reached their cage, the door was still open. They quickly ran inside.

"I hope that spider doesn't come in here," said Alex.

Everyone sat with their backs against the wall and faced the opened door. One by one, exhaustion overtook them, and they fell asleep. The next day, when they awoke, Celine could see that hall lights were back on but the energetic door was repaired.

"We're trapped again," she said, "While we were hiding from the spider, the door was repaired. We probably shouldn't have come back here."

"We had no choice," said Mando." Who knows what else is lurking out there."

Suddenly, Nina stood up. Celine noticed that her eyes seemed void of emotion.

Nina bent down beside the fountain and fished Alex's taser from the water and placed it on the dirt floor. Then she bent over the water and scooped up a handful and drank from her hands several times. Mando went down on his knees and joined her.

After she had drunk several handfuls, she turned and smiled at Celine, then Alex.

"Don't say anything," she whispered. "You'll make me cry and it won't be pretty."

Celine reached for Nina's hand and said, "You want to live. We all do."

For a moment, Celine felt sorry for all the nasty things she had said to Nina. Maybe Venera was right. Maybe, it was time to forgive.

Suddenly, Nina's eyes lit up.

"It's my sister," she said.

"Is it another recording?" asked Alex.

"No, she's coming through loud and clear," Nina said with joy.

"Anna, what's happening? Are the Space Warriors going to rescue us?"

"Yes, but I have Captain Orlove here," Anna said sadly. "He needs to speak with you."

"Hello, Nina. This is Captain Orlove."

"Hello," Nina said in a surprisingly timid manner.

"We have a very important job we want you to consider."

Nina continued listening. All the teens were listening to the conversation now and waited for Captain Orlove to finish speaking.

"We want to help you guys, but the only way the Warriors can dock on that ship is if you can stop it or slow it down."

"Yes," said Nina with trepidation in her voice.

"We need you to interface with a supercomputer."

Nina gasped, "No. I can't do that."

"Now Nina, I don't want you to freak out, but if we can send this signal from the computer to your implant, you could send that signal through the entire ship."

"So?" Nina said nervously.

"The signal is like sonar; it will bounce back images of everything in the ship."

"Pictures? You still want pictures?" Alex asked angrily.

"Hear him out," said Celine. "The photos might be needed for our rescue."

"Precisely," said the captain. He continued. "Nina, you will have a map of the entire spaceship. You'll know where the Command Station is. And once you get there, you could stop that ship."

Nina appeared flushed. Celine moved closer to her. She could see that Nina's aura was fading from a calm blue to green, which indicated fear and uncertainty.

"We've created a patch for your implant to help protect it from the vibrations, but I can't make any guarantees."

Nina closed her eyes.

"I'll have to think about it," she whispered.

"What do you mean, you'll think about it?" yelled Alex. "Why won't you do this?"

Nina looked down at her hands in her lap.

"I'm afraid," she simply said. "Afraid it might destroy me."

"I'm sorry, Nina," said Captain Orlove. "The patch does give you some protection, but I can't make any guarantees. If you won't do it, we'll try to come up with something else, but we don't have much time."

Celine reached for Nina's hand. Their eyes met.

"Nina, we might not get out of this alive if you don't take this chance. You're our only hope."

Nina closed her eyes again and took in a deep breath.

Reluctantly, she said, "Okay. I'll do it,"

Anna, on the Com, spoke up, "I love you, sister. Are you ready?"

"No. But I'm doing it anyway." Nina smiled with closed lips and teary eyes.

"I'm sorry I was so mean to you," she said to Celine.

"I forgive you," Celine said. Her mouth felt so dry and she could feel her own face feeling flushed. She didn't know it would be so easy to forgive Nina, but she felt the sincerity in Nina's words. *Grandmother would be proud of me.*

Captain Orlove's voice cracked. "I'm going to count to three and then the signals will be sent. Okay?"

"Okay," Nina sniffled and squeezed Celine's hand tightly. A few minutes after the signal was sent, Celine could feel a slight tingle from Nina's hand. She felt the pulse grow stronger and could only imagine how Nina, who was getting the full impact, must feel. Nina's eyes were closed, and it seemed like her entire body was quivering.

After about sixty seconds of the vibrations, it stopped. Nina opened her eyes in surprise.

"Was that it? Are you finished with me?"

"Yes," said the captain. "You did well. The data is coming in now. Do you need me to draw a map of the ship and resend it?"

"No, everything's in my download. I think I see the Command Center."

"Good. We'll stay in touch. Over and out."

Everyone was elated that Nina was okay and now had a map of the ship. She was their shero! The boys were ready to put Celine's plan into effect, but Nina was tired. Celine said it made sense to let her rest for a moment. She would need all her strength to do her part in Celine's plan.

After thirty minutes Nina got up, went to the hole in the floor and, to everyone's shock, peeled down an opening on her jumpsuit, squatted over the hole in the floor and urinated into it.

Mando stared wide-eyed and with his mouth open. Alex hit him on his arm.

"Turn your back. Look away," he said to Mando.

Mando turned his back to Nina. He was mesmerized by her and hadn't considered what was the gentlemanly thing to do. Nina fastened her clothes, rinsed her hands at the spigot above the makeshift toilet, walked robot-like to the trough of potatoes, then picked up one and ate it, green skin and all. She took two scoops of water and drank heartily. Then she stood tall; her face was tense, and her eyes hard. She spoke with the strength and conviction of a Samurai warrior.

"I'm ready! Let's work the plan!"

"That's my girl," said Mando with pride.

"Sure," said Nina. "Now let's kick that invisible giant's arse."

"Everyone ready?" asked Celine.

The teens all nodded yes.

"Okay, let's rock and roll," said Alex.

CHAPTER 17

PLAN :

CELINE'S PLAN

In the owner's quarters of the asteroid ship was a female Guardian, Drae. On her planet she was beautiful. Her ash-gray skin and muscular body made her a good catch for her husband, Draegon. However, they had more in common than their good looks. They were both scientists with a calling. They were called to save the Nimals of their universe. For hundreds of years, they had been traveling through space on their private ship, gathering up Nimals and plants and relocating them to hospitable planets. While in their care, they were fed nourishing roots and given the purest of water to drink. However, she was concerned about the last four Nimals they had acquired. Each had a metallic chip in their left wrist, which Drae's medical Bots promptly removed. One of them had a partial mechanical brain. She had never seen such a damaged being. The medical Bots were designing a full-body cocoon for her healing. She hoped it would work.

Poor little thing.

Her husband was going to be late for dinner. He said he was going to check on the new Nimals who were making loud noises. He wanted to make sure they were safe, and he didn't want the noise to disturb the other Nimals. He was gone so long, she wondered what mess he had gotten himself into. She remembered when they took in an innocent-appearing plant. It was beautiful, but it ate most of the other plants in the atrium before they realized it. They had to shoot it out into space to save the other plants.

She picked up her Com from the cabinet and called him.

"Oh my," she said when she heard his Com ring from his favorite chair. "I had better check on him."

Celine's plan went into action. Everyone started yelling, "We're hungry! Bring more food!"

Celine and Alex even banged on the side of the food trough, causing a loud noise and disturbing the other captives. She could hear some of them crying and running about in their cages. She continued to yell and bang as she watched the energized door. She saw the energy field at the entrance disappear and the light-being stepped into their cage. Then she immediately went into action.

"It's in here!" she shouted.

Nina and Mando jumped into a martial arts stance, legs wide and fists up.

"There!" she yelled and pointed toward the giant's head. "Twelve o'clock! Now, Nina!"

Nina jumped into the air and gave the giant her hardest kick ever to the head. Then Nina fell backward to the floor and held her foot.

"There's something there," she said in amazement. "And it's harder than concrete."

The giant slumped down slightly and held his head.

Celine signaled to Mando, pointing to the giant's bent-over body.

"Three o'clock! Hard!"

Mando kicked the giant in his rear end as hard as he had ever kicked.

"What the heck! Is it made of stone?" he said.

Celine ignored Mando but kept her eyes on the giant, who was now lying face down on the floor.

Getting cautiously closer but out of arm's reach, she looked for a place where Alex could put his tasers. Then she saw the giant's hands.

"Here," she said as she pointed to what appeared to be a hand with six fingers.

Alex took off one of his tasers and stuck it to a hand. The hand twitched. Celine pointed to the other six-fingered hand and Alex attached another taser.

"This should keep this thing incapacitated for a while," he said triumphantly.

Then he stood back.

"We did it!" cheered Celine. "Nina, lead the way."

Nina timidly stepped into the hall with everyone close behind her.

"You said we're supposed to turn right and go 300 meters. Remember?" said Mando.

"Of course, I do. I have a map of this entire ship encoded in my brain. Follow me."

Celine took another look at the giant lying motionless on the floor. She shuddered to think what it might do to them once it awoke.

"Look! There are more cages on this end of the ship."

"And we'll have to pass them to get to the Command Center," said Nina.

"They might be empty," said Celine.

Being the tallest and looking over everyone's head, Alex responded.

"No, none of them are empty and there are at least fifty going this route. Are you sure this is the only way to get to the Command Center?"

Nina nodded.

"Well, nothing serious happened when we passed them yesterday," said Mando.

"We only passed two cages yesterday," whispered Alex.

"Well, whoever is in them will not see us. We have to get to the Command Center. We've got to hurry," said Celine. "I don't want to look over my shoulder and see that giant behind us. Go, Nina. We got your back."

And as if remembering she was a Samurai leader, Nina spoke confidently.

"We need to stay close to the wall. Let's go and stay quiet."

They walked quickly and quietly passed several tinted glass windows. They avoided looking in and were focused on getting to the Command Center. But then they passed a window and felt compelled to stop. Behind the tinted glass, inside a room identical to the one they had escaped from, were people who looked very much like them. There were four teens—two boys and two girls—their skin a rich green. The captives had light brown hair and caramel-colored eyes. However, the boy's hair was short like Mando's and Alex's. Except for their green skin color, they looked like any normal teens.

The green people seemed preoccupied with drinking water and eating green potatoes but then the older girl stopped eating and began to sniff the air. The other girl did the same. The two girls moved closer to the window and held their heads high and wiggled their noses as if smelling the air. Then, as if they were scared rabbits, they ran back to the food to continue eating but cautiously.

Alex chuckled. "I think they could smell you, Mando."

"Let's keep moving," said Celine quietly.

As they passed another cage, they also felt compelled to stop. The teens in this cage almost seemed hypnotic. There were also two girls and two boys in the room. The teens were jet black, with dark eyes and black curly hair. They all wore identical solid white outfits.

Celine and Mando seemed hypnotized by their beauty.

"We're out here. Open the door," Celine and Mando began to mumble.

Celine walked toward the energized door, but Alex pulled her away.

"We don't have time for this," he told Celine.

He tapped her on the cheek.

"What are you doing," she asked, startled back into reality.

"You were talking out of your head. Like you were in a trance or sleepwalking," Alex told her.

"Sleepwalking?" Celine paused. "I hear her. That's the voice I heard when I almost drown on the engineer's repair bridge."

"That's creepy. We better get away from this cage before you do something silly."

"Mando, are you okay?" Alex asked.

Mando shook his head quickly.

"Yes. I'm okay, but what just happened?"

"I'm not sure, but it appears you and Celine were hypnotized. Let's go. We can't make any more stops. That giant might wake up and there might be more. Have you seen anything, Celine?"

"Don't jinx us. No, I haven't."

They passed the other cages quickly, all containing different human types; some with strange skin colors, some with elongated heads, different but all uniquely people-like. Mando and Nina seemed so surprised to see so many different beings.

If we weren't trying to escape, I would want to know these people, thought Celine.

"Amazing," Mando mumbled.

"Eventually, all of humanity will know the truth about extraterrestrials," whispered Celine.

At last, they got to the hall where they would turn left. Celine continued to look out for the giants but saw no signs of any. She hoped they would not be waiting for them in the Command Center.

At the end of the hall was an opening. Coming from the opening were buzzing sounds that reminded Celine of the noises that came from the Commons in the Martian Compound.

"Let me go in first so I can check it out," she said. The others stepped back to wait. She pressed her body against the wall and inched her way to the opening of the Command Station. Sliding down to the floor, she peeked through the opening while whispering a prayer for protection. She looked carefully at every inch of the surprisingly small room and did not see any energies to indicate there were living beings in the room. However, she did see six disgustingly ugly holographic workers who appeared gray with extreme musculature. *If the aliens look like these holograms they must be wearing camouflage, and I do not want to see them in person.*

The holograms were working at different consoles. Strangely, some of the consoles were on the walls and some were even on the ceiling and the holograms worked upside down. She turned to look at her friends, who were anxiously waiting for her report.

"There are only holograms in there," she said.

"How do you know that?" said Nina. "I can't tell them from real beings."

"They have no auras, and the light coming from their images is distorted."

Nina's eyes widened and then she shook her head to indicate she understood.

"I need to warn you. The holograms do not look like people from Earth.

They are extremely ugly. Just ignore them and they should ignore us."

"Wait," said Nina. "I need to let Anna know that we're entering the Command Center."

After speaking to her sister, she reached for Mando's hand and the two of them stepped into the room. Celine and Alex followed.

"Amazing," said Alex. He immediately began to check out a console that was not being used.

Nina, using her artificial eye as a camera, began to look at every part of the room from corner to corner. Finally, she received a message from the captain.

"There is a button above you," he said. "I've noticed that its location has changed several times."

Nina looked up; there was a console with three buttons over her head. She listened for other instructions.

"Push the button with the three triangles, the..." The Com became static. Then silence.

"Oh no. I think they're on to us," said Nina.

Celine heard heavy footsteps enter the room. She could feel the vibrations under her feet. There were two giants coming in quickly and heading for them. Quickly she moved to hide under the console and motioned for everyone to follow, but before she could get under the console one of the giants snatched her up by both of her arms. Alex saw Celine jerked upward and it appeared she was floating off to the hall. Then Nina was lifted and slung over something as if she was a sack of potatoes and floated out of the room.

"Celine!" Alex shouted and ran towards her.

But an electrified door now covered the opening to the Command Center and a force knocked him on his bottom. He and Mando were now trapped in the Command Center and Celine and Nina were gone.

CHAPTER 18

TAKEN

"Alex, are you alright?" shouted Mando as he raced toward Alex to help him.

"I'm okay." Alex rubbed his hip. The hair on his head stood up straight as if he had been playing with a Van-de Graaff.

"What just happened?" said Mando. "It was like something just snatched them up and took them out of here."

"I'm afraid we can't help them now," muttered Mando. His eyes slowly searched the room, looking for a way out of the Command Room. "We're trapped."

"No, there is help out there," said Alex as he looked up at the ceiling as if he could see into space. "The Warriors are waiting for us to do our part."

"Let's get back over there, we have to find the three triangles," he said. "Time is running out for us. Time might have already run out for the girls."

He almost choked on his words.

With feet dangling, Celine was carried into a room that was unnerving like the infirmary on The Fantasy. The walls and surrounding cabinets were white and pristine. Silver medical tools in metal trays covered a countertop next to a sink and faucet. She wanted to scream, but before she could open her mouth she was dropped onto an examining table.

She saw Nina taken into an adjacent room. She heard Nina scream once and then a loud purring sound began.

The light-being who dropped Celine said something that sounded like a bass singer, deep and intimidating, and suddenly his camouflage was gone and towering over her was the most hideous being she had ever seen. Its skin was chalky white or light gray. It was difficult to tell in the strangely lit room, but it reminded her of the armored texture of a cute armadillo. However, nothing about this extraterrestrial was cute. Its face was large and menacing. From it, large red eyes stared down at her. She wanted to close her eyes, to block out the sight that stood before her, but she could not close them. The menacing red eyes kept staring into hers as if looking for something. She could feel its warm breath on her face coming from two small slits where its nose should have been. Holding her breath, she leaned back from the being, but it moved in closer and grabbed her face with its muscular six-fingered hand. She could not move her head as it looked deeply into her eyes. One tear rolled slowly down her cheek. Then she heard what sounded like her grandma Enisi's voice.

"Do not be afraid, granddaughter."

For a moment Celine felt the warmth of her extended family surrounding her.

A female's voice startled her. It was deep and sounded like someone used to giving commands.

"Stop, Draegon. You are frightening her."

Celine could not tell if she had heard this with her ears or in her head. She looked up and saw another hideous being that was slightly taller than the one that had frightened her. Except for the height difference, they appeared identical.

The shorter ET, who was at least two and a half meters tall, stepped back in deferment to the taller one. He patted a blackish bruise mark on its forehead as if making certain Celine noticed it.

The ET that Celine had decided was female, and hopefully, the commander of the ship looked into Celine's eyes. Her eyes were also red, but Celine did not sense any anger from her.

"You are a unique Nimal," the female ET said to Celine. "You can see us when we don't want to be seen," it clucked. "You have something in your eyes. Does it help you to see us?"

Celine found the alien's voice to be calming, but the anger she felt from the other alien had not left her yet, so she was still fearful. *Something in my eyes?* Then she remembered her contacts. She had gotten so used to them, she forgot she had them in. *They don't help me see auras.*

As if the giant heard her thoughts and knew the contacts were of no help, it continued.

"Are there others like you?"

"Yes," Celine said as if she had to answer the giant's question. "My father."

The tall being said something to the short one. They both stared at each other and were silent. They appeared to be communicating but Celine could not hear them. Then the terrified teen noticed that neither of the space beings had ears! She tried to read their body language and auras, but up close their auras were like bright lights and very uncomfortable to stare at. Celine looked away and allowed her eyes to roam over the room, looking for a door or some way to get out of the room. She saw no signs of a door, no light distortions.

Somehow, she got the courage to face the feminine ET and asked, "Why did you bring us here?"

The female's long slit of a mouth turned upward like a smile and its eyes widened. It seemed surprise that Celine was trying to communicate with it.

I think she smiled.

Feeling a little more confident, Celine asked, "Where are you taking us?"

The masculine being seemed irritated that he did not know what Celine was saying, but the female appeared to understand. She turned to her partner and, in what Celine believed was a loving manner, repeated Celine's remarks in her own language.

Celine could hear it in her head. It sounded like a song, beautiful in contrast to their hideous appearances. Then the female turned to Celine.

"You will be saved," she said.

"Saved?" Celine said reflectively. "Saved from what?"

"Saved from extinction," replied the female.

Celine was confused. She remembered sitting on a couch, about to eat hot dogs and watch a new movie, when a bubble surrounded her and her friends and jetted them off to this asteroid ship. She didn't remember feeling in danger, until she awoke on their dirt floor.

The other alien began speaking or singing quickly. The female appeared to smile again.

"Draegon said you don't appreciate our efforts. You told your friends to beat him."

Celine did not want to look at the angry being, but she did and, as kindly as she could, she said, "I'm sorry we hurt you, but we want to go back to our ship."

She could not contain her emotions any longer. Tears rolled down her face and she sniffled.

"I was going to Earth to meet my grandmother."

"She is your family?"

"Yes."

"This makes you sad?" The alien seemed surprised that Celine had such emotions.

"I've never met her in person. She might transition soon. She might already be dead."

Celine could not hold back the flood of tears and she began sobbing out loud. She knew for certain she was abducted, possibly like all the other beings she saw in the glass cages; she was a prisoner with no real control over her life. Her abductors were not human, nothing about them appeared human. She wondered if they would understand how important it was for her to go back to The Fantasy, if they could sense her emotions and understand her.

Suddenly, the asteroid ship jerked and gave out a bellowing sound. Again a surprised look from the beings, raised areas where eyebrows should have been, crinkles on their hairless heads. Then they both said something in their language, then were camouflaged. Celine could see their bright auras around their camouflaged bodies. Then they disappeared before Celine's eyes. *It's those suits they're wearing that made them vanish,* she thought. She was relieved that they had left, but she now had new insight into what she and her friends were dealing with. In some ways they're like normal people with superior technology. Whether inferior or not, she hoped the Space Warriors' technology was enough to defeat them.

She climbed down from the table and peered into the room where they had taken Nina.

She didn't see her. In fact, nothing was in the room except a strange peanut-shaped box that made a purring sound. It was the size of a small person, a small person like Nina.

CHAPTER 19

TRAPPED

Mando spotted the button with the three triangles. He noticed they overlapped and created a nine-pointed star.

"Look at the button on the left," he said as he pointed to the upside-down console on the ceiling.

"Oh, I see it," said Alex. "It's an enneagram."

"Never heard of it," said Mando. "And now that we found it, how are we supposed to reach it? It looks like it's four meters high."

"Looks like everything in here is nailed down," said Alex, who had been looking for something to push under the console and climb on.

"You need to get on my shoulders," Alex told Mando.

"You can handle my weight?" stammered Mando, feeling a bit intimidated. Alex was only a few inches taller than him and, though he looked fit, Mando couldn't imagine Alex being that strong.

"I don't know. But I'm willing to try anything. That console must be very important, why else would it be on the ceiling? We've got to get to it and push that button."

Alex stooped down low and tensed his core muscles as Mando climbed onto his thigh and then onto his shoulders.

"This has to work the first time," Alex said with a shaky voice. He took a deep breath. "Because I won't be able to do this again."

With wobbly legs, Alex began to stand, lifting Mando, who was almost as big as him. When he finally stood up straight, his legs and shoulders were tense. Even the muscles in his face showed the strain of the weight he was lifting.

Then a worker hologram walked through Alex, who yelled, "That tickles!"

They both fell to the floor with Mando using his martial arts to break his fall with a roll.

"That's not going to work," said Mando. "I couldn't reach it, but I have an idea. I'm putting my arate training to use."

"Okay."

"I need you to stand here. I'm going to jump into your hands. You need to throw me upward and I'll do the rest."

"I don't know about this, but I'll try anything," said Alex.

Mando began doing cartwheels to warm up. Then suddenly flipped from Alex's hand and kicked the button.

"Darn!" yelled Alex, extremely impressed. "Man, you did it!"

Suddenly, all the holograms disappeared, and the ship went silent. Then the asteroid ship jerked and came to a hard stop as it made a bellowing noise.

"What's that awful noise?" said Mando. He stayed put on the floor, waiting for another hard jerk from the asteroid ship.

"Sounds like an injured moose," laughed Alex, who was so relieved that his conditioning for last year's Strong Man's Marathon had paid off in an unexpected way.

"It's the ship. I think we injured her," cried Mando. "Let's hope she won't retaliate."

Through a darkened window in the aliens' infirmary, Celine could see the blue auras of what appeared to be human beings in the hall. She hoped her mind was not playing tricks on her.

She thought she could hear herself scream, "Help me, please."

"Move away from the wall," a man shouted.

Celine moved to the back of the room just in time, as a hand-held particle disruptor blasted through the wall. A few sparks brightened the room and then the wall disintegrated.

There in front of her were three Space Warriors dressed in armor and carrying particle disruptors over their shoulders.

"Thank Spirit," Celine said as a flood of emotions washed over her.

"That's one of the missing girls," said the female warrior who had the photos of the missing teens.

"I'll get her back to the ship, ma'am," volunteered one of the Warriors.

He slung his weapon toward his back before helping Celine to her feet.

"You'll need to walk behind me," he said. "Can you do that?"

"Yes," she whispered. She was so overjoyed she thought she might faint.

Celine was ready to follow the Warrior. He appeared to be a few years older than Alex. He looked at her with suspicion and fear in his eyes. She could only imagine what he had seen in the alien's ship.

"Wait," she said. "My friend, Nina. I think she's in a box in that room. I tried to open it, but I couldn't."

Celine pointed to the room. Then followed the Warriors to the human-size box.

"Earlier, the box was purring," Celine said.

"It stopped just as we came in," said one of the Warriors.

Suddenly the lid popped open and lying inside the cocoon-like interior was Nina. She appeared to be asleep. Celine noticed right away that her aura was changed. Where there had been distortion was now whole.

The Warrior lifted her from the box.

"Let's head to the ship."

"Do you know where the boys are?"

"No, but I last saw them in the Command Room."

"Warriors are already headed there," he said to Celine. "Follow me."

As she followed him, she noticed that the hall appeared to have been changed. Where she had originally seen glass windows to rooms filled with many human-like beings, she now saw solid white walls and no sign of the glass cages.

"Everything is different," she told the soldier who quickly moved through the hall toward a tunnel that led to the docked Space Force spaceship.

"I need to get you two safely into our custody," he replied. "Tell the commanding officer everything you know once you are on board our ship."

Warriors, with particle disruptors drawn, had headed to the Command Station.

"This is an amazing piece of technology. If we could capture it imagine what the engineers could do with it," mumbled Captain Orlove.

"It's a rescue mission first," said his second in command.

"Whoa! Will you look at that," one of the Warriors whispered as he nodded his head toward the rows of glass cages.

"Are people in them?"

"I'm not sure," one soldier said as he got closer to one of the cages to get a better look.

Suddenly, he began to mumble, "Open the door. Let us out."

He began walking quickly, heading toward the end of the cage where he hoped to find a door. Another Warrior ran after him and grabbed his arm just as he was about to touch a keypad next to the cage.

"Jeff, wait a minute, what are you doing? You know this is against protocol."

"Jeff, Jeff," the other Warrior called. "What's wrong with him?"

"Captain, he's in some kind of trance."

Captain Orlove quickly ran down the hall where the Warriors were trying to wake Jeff out of his trance. He took one look at Jeff and punched him hard in the face.

"Ouch! Why did you do that, Captain?" asked Cadet Jeff.

"You were wasting our time," said the captain.

Then an eerie screeching sound rang through the halls, so loudly that the Warriors covered their ears and closed their eyes in pain. When they opened their eyes, the glass walls had transformed into what appeared to be solid white walls, and the soldiers could no longer see the young captives.

"I don't like this place," said Jeff. "It's playing tricks on my mind. The sooner we get out of here, the better."

"We need to quickly find Alex and his friends, and get out of here before it's too late," said the lieutenant.

"Yes," said Captain Orlove. "We have a team looking for them. They've already located the girls. Now we need to find that Command Room."

Suddenly the ship shook, and it felt like it was moving again.

"You feel that?" asked Jeff.

"Yeah. The ship's moving. We don't have much time," said the captain.

CHAPTER 20

EARTH AND MARS SPACE FORCES

"I think the alien is in here," Alex said. "It's camouflaged, but I remember that strong meat lab scent."

"Yeah, "I can smell it too."

Both boys began to back away from the scent.

"Let go of me," yelled Mando.

Alex saw that Mando's arms were pinned behind his back, and he was struggling to free himself. Then he felt cold hard hands grab both of his wrists. At that point, he felt a powerful push forward toward the energized door. Alarmed that he would be electrocuted, Alex pushed his heels down to stop himself from moving, but he continued to be pushed forward. He noticed that Mando was also being pushed toward the door. He braced himself for what he imagined would be excruciating pain. But when they reached the door, the pushing stopped, and Alex heard a harsh voice behind him say something that sounded like 'Drek!'

Then he felt air from the hall rush into the room and standing before him was the most welcomed sight, three Space Warriors with their weapons drawn. Alex felt his wrists released and he darted into the hall and Mando was right behind him.

However, before Mando could get into the hall, the door reenergized and zapped him on the heel causing him to fall.

"Ouch! That hurt," he said as he sat on the floor beside the captain.

"Are you boys okay?" asked the Captain as everyone gathered around Mando.

"I'm okay," Mando said. "But you've got to help us find the girls. The aliens took them."

"Don't worry. We have the girls. They're on our ship," said the captain. "What just happened? I heard a zap when you yelled."

"They have energized doors that can knock you out," said Alex when he noticed the captain eyeing the glass wall at the entrance to the alien's Command Center. "It might be powerful enough to kill you."

"So, we can see in there, but can't get in there? Darn it! said the frustrated captain.

He then turned to his Second Lieutenant, "You and Jeff take these boys back to the ship. I have something I need to do here."

"Sir?" asked Jeff. "We can't leave you alone on this ship. That's against all protocol."

"Who are you to speak to me of protocol? You heard your orders."

"We did sir," said the second lieutenant. "Let's go Cadet," he said to Jeff.

"Where's the ship?" asked Alex. "We don't have any protective wear."

"You won't need any," said the cadet. We laser-burned a hole right to the core of this fake asteroid. Our ship is on the surface, right above the tunnel and we have MMOD shielding between the tunnel and our ship."

"There are other people on this ship. We saw them in cages," said Mando. "Can we set them free?"

"We will do what we can," said the cadet assuredly. However, Alex noticed that the second lieutenant smirked.

The boys bustled together between the two Warriors as they headed for the Warriors' spaceship.

"Everything looks different now," said Mando as they cornered one of the halls of the aliens' ship. "What happened to the cages?"

"We're not sure," said the cadet. "We saw walls appear out of nowhere to hide them. It's a good thing we have a beacon on our ship, or we'd never find our way out of here."

"Cadet," said the second lieutenant as he gave him a stern look that Alex interpreted as 'Shut your mouth.'

The cadet bit his lip. "No more questions," he said. "Keep moving."

So, the boys and the Warriors walked silently and quickly, unimpeded, through the quiet halls, following the beacon to their ship.

Finally, they reached the laser-created tunnel. It sloped upward toward the warrior's spaceship. Sitting above the tunnel, waiting on the surface, was their rescuer. Alex remembered that his dad had practically given the spaceship to Earth Space Force which had been incorporated into the makings of a new military spaceship.

"It seems a lot bigger than I remembered," said Alex as he looked up at the bottom of the Warriors ship.

"It is," mumbled the cadet.

"Wow! Wouldn't my dad be surprised that his old ship would be used to rescue me from an alien abduction."

The boys and warriors climbed the shiny metal steps through an opening beneath the ship into the sanitation area. Neither Alex nor Mando had bathed since they had been abducted four days ago.

"Glad to get out of these filthy clothes," said Alex. "They will never be clean enough for me to ever wear again."

"Dito that," said Mando.

After everyone had been sprayed with a soapy solution and then rinsed with water, they were given a strong blue light shower and then deemed safe to intermingle with some of the crew on the ship. Alex and Mando were given clean Karate suits from the warriors' gym. Then had a meal of steak and potatoes in the mess hall. At last, they were taken to the infirmary where the girls had been confined. When the boys entered the infirmary, Alex saw Celine sitting in a chair in a corner of the room. She seemed immersed in a book titled *Lost in the Red Hills of Mars* and Nina was sleeping in a bed on the other side of the room. When Celine saw the boys, her face lit up and she ran straight to Alex's arms, giving him a big hug.

"You're alive," she squealed.

"Yes, we are," said Mando.

"Thank the Great Spirit," said Celine and then gave Mando a hug. He gloated.

"You did it! she said to both boys. "And we're going to Earth! And the doctor said this ship can get us there before the Fantasy. Isn't that wonderful! I can get to Earth in time to meet my grandmother."

Then to Celine's surprise, Nina sat up in her bed and said loudly, "We ALL did it."

Celine turned to face Nina. Four days earlier, before she had been abducted, she wouldn't have felt the love and compassion she was feeling for Nina at that moment. She ran over to Nina's bedside and embraced her.

"You're going to be okay," she cried and then kissed her on her cheek.

"Group hug," said Alex as he and Mando ran over and jumped on Nina's bed to give her and Celine a group hug.

Meanwhile, inside the alien ship, the captain tried to neutralize the energy wall that kept him from the Command Center. He played various tones he had recorded on his Com system. The engineers had given him these musical tones that they had obtained from the mechanical fly. They had reversed-engineered the fly, but none of the tones had any effect on the glass wall.

The aliens were no longer camouflaged, and the captain watched as they tinkered with a console located on the ceiling.

"You don't frighten me," he mumbled. He had been in the Space Force for several years, and though the average citizens of Earth didn't believe in extraterrestrials, he had seen at least fifty different species but had no clearance to share this knowledge, not even with his wife.

He demonized them as he thought about how he would confiscate their ship.

"Darn, I've never seen anything as ugly as you. You lazy slow-moving sloths," he shouted.

The aliens continued intensely working at the console and ignored his insults and his attempts to get into their Command Center. Then the larger alien ambled over to a console that jutted from a wall while the other continued working at the ceiling console. It seemed to smile at him, and for a moment he thought he heard a female say, *"Naughty boy."*

"I'm taking this ship," hissed the captain. "And you'll have no way to stop me."

Then he heard a loud bellowing sound and both aliens looked at him, their lipless mouths turned up in a smile. For a moment, he felt like a child being scolded by his parents.

The captain yelled with anger, "You gray boneheads won't be smiling when I release this particle disruptor and blow this ship to smithereens. Then my men will vacuum you up and this precious ship into a five-kilogram canister."

He knew this self-imposed mission was dangerous and could possibly put his own ship at risk, but he had to take that chance. Everything about this ship was special, built to look like an asteroid, a treasure trove of different technology. He had decided before arriving to the aliens' ship that the Earth Space Force should have this technology and he would take it by any means necessary. He sat a disruptor next to the energized wall. He would detonate the disruptor from his ship once they had lifted off and were in what he believed would be the safety zone.

Suddenly he could feel the alien ship moving. He hurriedly put in his authorization code and thumbprint, then he left the area, running back through the halls and up the tunnel to his spaceship. No one tried to intercept him as he left and he was a little disappointed that it was so easy, so defenseless. He thought the aliens were either afraid of the warriors or didn't believe the warriors had the technology or the will to hurt them. They must not have had many dealings with Earth.

"Let's get out of here," he said to his team once he was on board his spaceship.

"Captain, something is wrong with the electronics. Everything is going haywire. We can't lift off," said the pilot.

The captain looked at the console and saw the numbers on the dashboard were moving erratically as if counting backward instead of forward.

Then a terrifying scraping sound, like metal moving across metal, permeated their ship and then their ship slid a few meters.

"Captain, take a look at this!" shouted another Warrior who had been monitoring the tunnel for a possible attack from the aliens.

The captain along with several other Warriors hurried toward the screen that showed the asteroid ship below them.

"What is it doing?" asked the captain.

"I'm not sure, sir. But it looks like the asteroid is healing itself, sir."

"Healing itself?" The captain's eyes widened. "You don't think it'll swallow this ship, do you?" he asked as he went back to check the navigation console. The numbers on the panel were still moving backwards.

"The dirt and rocks have shifted and are closing the hole—I mean the tunnel—we carved into it."

The ship swayed and then slipped off the asteroid into space and began drifting powerless towards Mars.

"Any weapon signatures?" asked the captain nervously.

"No, sir, but the asteroid ship is heading toward the Asteroid Belt."

"Captain," said the navigator. "We have control of the Board now."

"How far away is the asteroid ship," asked the captain.

"It's twenty-one Kilometers, sir."

"We got you now!" he yelled at the asteroid ship as it headed toward the asteroid belt. With glee in his eyes, he typed out the detonation code for the particle disruptor.

"Unable to detonate," said the AI in charge of the disruptors.

"What?" cried the captain.

"Unable to detonate," repeated the AI.

"Sir, this has never happened before," the Warrior at the console said. "The asteroid ship is pulling out of range."

The captain watched as the alien ship with all its wonderful technology glided into the asteroid belt, and then disappeared as it passed Ceres.

"Waiting for your orders, sir," said the pilot.

"Try the code again," said the captain.

"Target out of range," said the AI.

"Let's get out of here," said the captain in disappointment. "We got what we came here for."

"But, sir, they have our disruptor! They have our technology now."

"What good is it to them?" yelled Captain Orlove. "Let's leave this place for Artemis.

Mr. Rittenhouse is waiting for his son and friends."

"Setting a course for Artemis," said the pilot.

Then he put his codes into his dashboard and a wormhole, a shortcut through time and space, formed at the nose of the warriors' ship like an energized tunnel of flashing lights and heat in the middle of the black universe. The Earth Space Force ship entered the wormhole that it had created, and like a giant electric monster, the wormhole appeared to swallow the ship, leaving only darkness behind.

CHAPTER 21

THE INTERROGATION

"We're going to arrive on the moon before the Fantasy does," said Alex.

"How do you know that?" asked Mando. He shifted his weight on the hard bed in the infirmary.

"Cadet Jeff told me. He said my dad is waiting there for us."

"We're going straight to the moon?" whined Nina. "Look at me. I don't want to go to the moon looking like this!"

Like the boys, she and Celine were wearing Karate suits.

"This suit's too large"

She shook her arms and the sleeves fell pas her hands.

"Why can't we just go to the Fantasy first?"

"You look beautiful," said Mando.

Nina rolled her eyes at Mando. "I want my things!" she said.

"Don't worry about your things. I'm sure they're safe on the Fantasy," said Alex. "Besides, I'll treat everyone to the latest outfits on the moon."

Celine noticed Nina perked up at the mention of a new outfit. *How quickly Earthlings get back to being their usual selves.* A new outfit wasn't going to perk Celine up. She had not spoken to any of her family since the kidnapping and she didn't know how her grandmother had fared or if she was still alive.

Just then a Warrior peeked through the window of the infirmary. He spoke to the teens from behind glass.

"You are not to discuss the events of the past four days with anyone. Do you understand?"

The teens looked at each other in surprise, but neither of them responded to the question.

The Warrior continued, "When we arrive at Artemis, you will be kept in quarantine and interrogated."

"Yes," said Alex as if he was speaking for everyone.

Then the Warrior left as quickly as he had appeared.

Celine said, "Why does he want to interrogate us? We haven't done anything wrong."

"I'm sure he simply meant to say question us," said Alex.

"I don't know about that. He looked extremely serious when he said interrogate," said Mando.

"I just want to get to my family," said Nina.

"Me too," said Celine.

The teens were kept in the infirmary for the duration of the trip. As soon as the ship came out of the wormhole, it flew directly into an underground tunnel on the moon that led to the Earth Space Force Headquarters. After the ship had docked, the teens were ushered to the medical facility on the base where they were X-rayed, and full body images were taken of them. After each of the teens was questioned by a psychiatrist and hypnotherapist, they were told to wait in a conference room together until they had a final interview with personnel from the World Federation.

They all sit silently, robot-like, in the conference room, seemingly stunned by their physical tests and the results. Finally, Celine broke the silence.

"My identity chip was gone from my arm," said Celine.

"Mine too," said Mando and Alex.

"But I was told that our health and school history can be retrieved and placed on a new implant."

"Wonderful," said Mando. "I would hate to think I had taken double loads of classes for nothing."

"What about you, Nina? Did the aliens take your implant too?" asked Celine.

Nina laughed. "Yes, they took it. And my Brain-Computer Interface."

"What? How is that possible?" said Mando. "How do you feel?"

"Never felt better. The psychologist gave me an IQ test and I'm just as smart as my twin sister."

Nina raised her eyebrows. "I used to be smarter than my sister."

"I thought you wanted to be normal," said Mando.

"All my life I wanted to be normal. Now that I'm, I'm not so sure anymore. Being normal is overrated. Isn't it, Celine?"

Celine shook her head 'yes'. It made her think about herself and how she had wanted to be a normal Earth girl. How badly she had wanted to be like the twins. At this moment, she was glad to be alive and made a promise that she would appreciate herself, weird eyes too. After all, it was the abnormal parts of her and Nina that facilitated their rescue.

"Who are we waiting to speak with?" asked Mando.

"Personnel from the World Federation," said Alex. "Not many people get to sit down with members of the World Federation," he continued. "They're very powerful people."

"Aren't they like the old CIA and KGB all rolled into one?" said Mando.

"Somewhat. Those organizations did shadowy things for the survival of their countries, but the World Federation does shadowy things for the survival of Planet Earth," replied Alex.

"Shadowy things? I wonder why they need to speak with us," said Celine.

"Like cover ups," said Nina. "This is where we'll get the real interrogation."

"I have nothing new to add to my story," said Celine.

"It's a little more complex than that," said Alex.

Celine couldn't understand the nuances of what Alex or Nina said, but before she could ask questions a female Warrior came into the waiting room.

"You will each have your interview with a Federation member. Be honest, and everything will go well for you."

She paused. "Which one of you is Nina?"

Nina swallowed hard. "I am," she said.

"You're first."

Nina stood up slowly. She had that 'why me' look on her face as she left the waiting room with the lady. In the hall, Nina was told to step into the room labeled C. When she opened the door, she was pleasantly surprised that the interviewer appeared to be a traditional Samurai. He was dressed in a reddish orange Akome, like ancient nobility.

"Konnichiwa," she said, and bowed as regally as she could in her over-sized karate suit.

"Konnichiwa," said the man. "You are from an honored family."

"Yes," Nina said with pride.

"You may be seated."

She noticed the chair was very old and was intricately carved from wood. It was polished to a beautiful shine.

"I am honored," she said, and sat very gently in the extravagant chair.

"One day, your family will hire a matchmaker to find you a suitable mate.

He would want to know that you are of good genes."

Nina's eyes began to water. "I am from the Emoto family. Our history is old and rich," she said.

"True, but you have the BCI."

Nina looked away. Her quivering chin was held high, and her watery eyes dried quickly.

"No, I do not have it anymore. Somehow, I am cured."

"Oh," said the man. "This will make my job easier."

Perched delicately on the fragile chair, Nina wondered if the man hadn't heard her. She continued listening, wondering where this talk was going.

"My personal matchmaker will be able to find you a future husband with high pedigree. However, if you are telling people you were abducted by some little green men, it will be challenging for her. Do you understand?"

Slowly, Nina's eyes warmed, and a faint smile was on her lips. "Yes. I do."

"In this case, silence is golden," he said.

Not in a hundred lifetimes did she think she would receive such an amazing offer, but now that she was a normal person she wondered if she truly wanted to be Traditionally Matched with anyone. She decided she would make that decision when she needed to.

"Silence is golden," she repeated. "I have no need to spread strange stories that I cannot prove."

The man nodded in agreement and said, "Now you may leave."

Celine noticed when Nina and the lady returned to the waiting room, Nina seemed happy, but in deep thought. When Nina was seated, the lady called Mando's name. He quickly stood up and followed her into the hall. He was told to go into the room with the letter B on its door.

When he entered the room, a man introduced himself as Dr. Laghari. He said he was a professor, and head of the Communication Department at the World Media University.

Mando shook the man's hand and sat in the chair across from Dr. Laghari.

Mando thought all the good things he had done in his short life were coming back to him in the form of this well-deserved visit.

"Our school is very interested in you," said Dr. Laghari. "We even have scholarship money available for you."

Mando's eyes lit up, but before he could say thank you Dr. Laghari continued.

"Of course, this offer would be removed if you were to bring any controversy to our fine university."

"Why would I do that?" asked Mando. "I have always been an upstanding student, not ever in any kind of trouble."

"You have had a unique experience this past four or five days."

The man waited for Mando to respond.

"Yes sir, I have. But what does that have to do with me getting the scholarship or being a student at the World Media University?"

"Our graduates are highly respected in the field of journalism. Some have received awards for outstanding journalism. People trust and respect what they say."

Finally, Mando was able to see the connection between his alien abduction and him not getting the scholarship.

"I understand," said Mando as he twisted uncomfortably in his chair. "Attending the World Media University is a great honor. Only the finest can attend. I have already forgotten my kidnapping experience. I will make you, your university, and my family proud."

"Then we will see you in the fall. Let me walk you out," said the man.

"Thank you, sir," Mando said as he left the room.

When Mando entered the waiting room, he seemed overjoyed. His eyes were bright and dreamy.

He smiled at Celine. "My dreams are coming true," he said.

"So are mine," said Nina, and she nodded at Mando with a serene smile on her face.

"Wow! You guys look pretty happy after your interviews. I can't wait to meet my interviewer," said Alex. "Am I next?"

"Yes, you are," said the lady who was waiting at the door.

Alex entered a room labeled A, where a man dressed in business attire waited for him. He introduced himself as a government official. He had Alex's business license for his Media Adventure Show in his hand. Alex took the seat in front of the man.

"Do you know what this is?" he asked Alex as he held it high, almost at Alex's eye-level.

"It looks like a business license," Alex said nonchalantly.

"I have your license renewal," he said.

Alex had been having difficulty renewing his media license. Since his experiences in the Martian Cave he hadn't been very adventurous, and hadn't produced the required number of adventure shows for the owners of the Media Platform.

"I see. Why?" Alex asked as he stared with a straight face, showing no emotion.

"We are trying to decide if we want to renew your license."

With unblinking eyes, Alex stared into the man's eyes and waited for the man to continue.

"You have breached your contract with Smith Media Corporation."

"There's no breach. I still have a month to produce the shows," said Alex, but he knew it was nearly impossible to produce five shows in four weeks.

"Suppose I could convince the company to let you keep the contract and give you more time to produce the shows."

"What's in it for you?"

The man didn't answer the question but said, "There was never an alien abduction. It never happened."

Alex chuckled when he realized what the man wanted from him.

"What are you talking about? What abduction?"

Both Alex and the man began to laugh.

"You're a good one," he said.

"I supposed I heard incorrectly."

"Yes, you did. I expect you will send my license and extend my contract for four additional months—free of late fees or charge for this imposition."

"Sure thing."

"Glad to know we're on the same page."

Alex stood up and shook the man's hand before leaving. *Wow, that's a load off my mind. I can get those shows completed easily in four months.*

Alex was exuberant when he returned to the waiting room.

"You're up next, Martian Girl," he said to Celine. "I hope you get what you want."

Celine noticed everyone seemed happy when they returned, but they also seemed somewhat different. She couldn't quite put her finger on it. It was like they were happy but had changed, and not necessarily in a good way.

The lady Warrior led Celine to the last room of the interview suites. She opened the door and asked Celine to step in. Celine smiled nervously and entered the room. She was surprised to see a friendly, friendly-faced female waiting to speak with her.

The woman said she was Ms. Green, from a prestigious leadership academy called the American Leadership Academy."

"We are looking forward to you attending one of our schools," she said. "We have small classes, one on one tutoring and many other amenities I'm sure you would enjoy. There you could make life time friends."

"That sounds wonderful," beamed Celine. "Do you have an academy in Hawaii?"

"Ahh." Ms. Green placed her hand on her left ear as if pushing something into it. Then she nodded. "Yes. We have an academy on the Big Island."

"My mom lives there! But I'll have to check with my mom first."

"Yes, certainly you'd want to talk with your mom first. I'm sure she would want you to attend our academy, one of the best in the US."

Ms. Green cleared her throat and spoke a little louder. "Don't know why I didn't know about Hawaii."

Celine chuckled. "Maybe it's because I didn't tell you."

Ms. Green raised an eyebrow, then looked toward the large mirror on the wall. She cleared her throat and then continued.

"It is still important to you to fit in with all the other students. Am I correct?"

"It was, but not anymore. It's more important to be myself. And to love me, flaws and all."

Mrs. Green stared at the mirror again. This time Celine stared at the mirror, too. She also smoothed her hair. Looked at both sides of her face. Decided she looked great despite the oversized karate suit she was wearing. Then she returned her attention to Ms. Green and smiled.

"Surely, you'd want to fit in with all the other students. Sometimes teens can be cruel to people who are different," Ms. Green said with a hint of aspiration in her voice. Celine wondered if Ms. Green was testing her.

So she replied, "I can't control how others behave. I can only control how I react."

Ms. Green was speechless. And since Ms. Green didn't say anything, Celine continued, "Right now I feel really happy with myself, and I don't care if I ever fit in."

Again, Celine waited for Ms. Green to speak, but Ms. Green seemed tongue-tied.

"May I leave now?" Celine said as she stood up, ready to head for the door.

"No!" Ms. Green shouted.

Celine widened her eyes in surprise at how desperately loud the round-faced lady sound. Her voice didn't match her friendly face.

"I mean not yet," said Ms. Green with less vigor. "Please, sit down."

Celine stared at the mirror for a moment, then returned to her seat.

"If you tell people you were abducted by aliens, they will think you're not in your right mind."

Celine whispered, "I know."

"Some teenagers can be really cruel."

Celine whispered again, "I know."

"Why are you whispering?" whispered Ms. Green.

Celine moved in a little closer toward Ms. Green.

"Someone is behind the mirror, listening to us."

Ms. Green sat back, wide-eyed.

"Are you certain?"

Celine nodded yes.

"I saw the aura behind the mirror."

"Oh! Well, in that case, I'd better whisper, too. You shouldn't tell anyone you were abducted because they will probably make fun of you, or even worse," Ms. Green whispered.

"You've already told me that," whispered Celine. "Is that all?"

"Yes," whispered Ms. Green. "Thank you for coming in today."

"You're welcome."

When Celine left the room, the psychiatrist who had been watching all the interviews with the teens entered the room from behind the mirrored wall.

"What an interesting girl," said Ms. Green to the psychiatrist.

"Yes, we weren't expecting that. I forgot about those eyes."

"I found her refreshingly innocent," whispered Ms. Green. "She's not a threat to the status quo."

"I don't know. It bothered me that we couldn't pinpoint what she wanted."

"Maybe she just wants to be herself."

"I don't care. She's the one to watch and if she ever says anything, it would be easy to discredit her."

"Do as you wish."

Back in the waiting room, Nina rushed to hug Celine.

"Did you get what you wanted?" Nina asked.

"No. They couldn't give me back my good name," Celine said longingly.

This caught Nina off guard. She felt like she had been slapped in the face. Already she had forgotten about the lie she and her sister had told to get Celine in trouble. She stepped back from Celine.

"Celine, I'm so sorry. I'll try to fix it," she promised.

CHAPTER 22

MARTIANS ON EARTH

The teens were released into Mr. Rittenhouse's custody, who then took them shopping for clothes and then to one of the moon's finest restaurants where they ordered anything they wanted and stuffed themselves until they could eat no more. After the restaurant, he took them to the most luxurious and only hotel on the heavenly body where they would stay and wait for the Fantasy to arrive. The time at the hotel went by quickly, and even though all of their time was spent indoors, something like on Mars, staying at the hotel was much more fun with lots of entertainment, and very good food.

All the teens were happy to see the Fantasy come in, and the guests on the Fantasy were happy to know that the teens were safe. The guests did not know the details of the teens' abduction, most assumed that they had been kidnapped and Alex and his friends were ransomed for millions of credits from Alex's dad, Mr. Rittenhouse.

Dr. Vee, the only one from the ship who had surmised the truth, wasn't so sure anymore. He had never heard of anyone escaping the Guardians. Nonetheless, he was elated to learn that the teens were safe on Lunar, Earth's moon, in the city of Artemis. When he finally saw them, he hugged each of them tightly as he cried sincere tears of joy.

Upon seeing Alex, Mr. Abiola apologized profusely for not keeping Alex safe. He even volunteered to resign from his job, but Alex wasn't having it.

"No one could have predicted a space kidnapping," said Alex who was determined to keep his alien abduction a secret. Besides, Mr. Abiola had worked for the family for a decade, since Alex was a little boy, and he didn't want a new bodyguard.

Celine remembered how Mr. Abiola's size and appearance had frightened her but compared to the aliens now he just looked like a gentle giant.

When the Smiths came out of the elevator that led to the docking station, Celine noticed Nina went over to them. She must have said something about Celine because they looked in her direction and smiled.

Everyone heard Anna when she got off the elevator, screaming her sister's name as she ran toward her. But when Venera came into the station, she ran straight to Celine and wrapped her arms around her. One would have thought Celine was her little sister.

"You poor girl," she said to Celine. "You've been through so much. I'm so glad you're safe."

Suddenly Celine remembered where she had seen Venera's face. The beautiful woman in the armor that was painted on the cave wall on Mars. When Celine told Venera, Venera exhaled loudly and began to cry.

"I didn't mean to upset you," Celine said. She rubbed her hands together, not knowing what to do or say next.

"These are tears of joy," Venera said. "For centuries, the stories about my family's escape from Mars had been told among us. Now I know it's true."

Venera patted her eyes dry with the sleeve of her jacket and gave Celine a weak smile.

"Thank you," she whispered. "We'll talk later."

Then she headed to the hotel that was conveniently connected to the docking area and shopping mall.

"Celine Red Cloud!" the loudspeaker called. "Please return to the Fantasy."

Celine had already headed to the ship when she heard the announcement. She knew she needed to get her things from her suite, especially her antique flute and Puggie. She had missed him so much. When she entered the Fantasy, she was surprised to find one of the ship's administrators waiting for her in her suite.

He said, "I have some good news about your grandmother. Your uncle called a few days ago. He wanted you to know that your grandma had the heart pump surgery and is doing well."

"Thank the Great Spirit," Celine said with relief.

" I also want to give you more good news. Breaking of Privacy Code 303 has been expunged from your records. It is no longer recorded in your ID chip and Alex's credits have been returned to his account."

Celine looked down at her left wrist where her ID chip had been removed by the aliens.

"I no longer have an ID chip," she said. "I don't know if I want a replacement."

"I see," said the surprised administrator. "Well, I'll make the changes in the super- computer. Your records will be there when you need them."

"Thank you. My parents will be very happy to know this."

"I'm happy, too," said the administrator. "So glad Nina Emoto came forward with the truth. Now her parents have been charged that fine, not yours. Justice has been served."

Celine nodded yes.

"Well, if you have no questions for me, I plan to join everyone on Lunar. Let me carry your things."

"I can manage. I don't have very much." *But I do have all that I need.*

"Okay. I hope you enjoy your new life on Earth."

"Thank you. I'm sure I will."

I'm not worried about Earth anymore. If I can survive an alien abduction, living on Earth will be a walk in the garden. Celine chuckled. *I think I said that correctly.*

As Celine was leaving the ship, she stood in the entrance where she had sadly said goodbye to her dad and step-mom. Her trip was supposed to have been a routine trip from Mars to Earth. Nothing about the trip turned out to be what she had anticipated. It had been quite an adventure; one she wouldn't want to experience again, despite the lessons she learned about herself and her friends. She wondered what adventures Earth would offer her, but no matter what, she knew that she would be strong and courageous enough to face anything. This was not the first time her unusual eyes had saved her, and it probably wouldn't be the last.

That evening in Hotel Artemis, Dr. Vee, on behalf of the Fantasy, gave a farewell party.

Dr. Vee was dressed in his colorful coat, and he danced around the room, hugging and kissing everyone.

"The crew and I are going to miss you," he said. "See, even the Bots will miss you."

The Valet Bots flew over to each of the guests that they had served and gave them fresh flowers from the ship's garden. Celine's bot handed her red roses. She smelled them and then joined in the party fun.

"Hey, Nina," she confidently called out when Nina entered the ballroom. "Show me how to do the dance that you taught Mando."

Nina gave Celine a thumbs up. Celine blew her a kiss and mouthed the words *thank you.*

Nina told the Hollows, as she had named the band, to play Hogaku. Instantly, the hologram band members began playing drums and bamboo flutes. Nina and Mando began the beautiful flowing dance that Celine had loved so much. She was standing on the sideline, clapping her hands to the beat of the drum when Alex walked over to her and asked her to be his dance partner. She cheerfully accepted. Then everyone joined the dance, gliding across the dance floor like floating Bots.

As Celine glided across the dance floor, she was no longer worried about pleasing the twins or wondering when they would accept her friendship. She didn't even worry about her awkwardness on the dance floor. She was happy. Happy to know her grandmother was alive, and she would meet her. Happy that she would live with her mom on Earth for two years. But most importantly, just plain happy to be Celine, an outback Martian girl.

"This is the best party ever," she said as she accidentally stepped on Alex's foot.

CHAPTER 23

THE ARTEMIS EXPERIENCE

Later that day Celine's mother and uncle arrived. They both wanted to know everything about the kidnapping. Like the Fantasy guests, they had been told that she and her friends had been rescued from pirates. Celine told them that she would give them all the details later. Right now, she didn't want to think or talk about it.

"No one hurt us and we're all fine," she said.

Her mom agreed and said, "You can talk about it when you're ready."

She held both of Celine's hands. Her mom's eyes were puffy, as if she had been crying.

"The important thing is no one was physically hurt. We'll get through this together," she said.

"I know," Celine said softly.

She wondered when she'd ever be ready to talk about it. Being abducted by aliens was not something that she could share with just anyone. She knew she wanted to tell her parents, but not yet. It was too soon to talk about it, still unnerving.

Her uncle, who looked like a younger version of her dad, told her that the family had convinced Grandma Enisi to get a partial mechanical heart transplant. She would have it until her new stem-cell-grown heart would be ready for her in a few months. She was doing well and looking forward to meeting her.

Her mom said they would be leaving for Earth in the morning. When they asked her what she thought of the view of Earth, they were surprised to learn that she had been spending all her time in the hotel and mall which were underground and hadn't gone up the tower to see Earth floating in Space. For some reason, she felt safer in the underground city.

However, after her mom had dropped off her suitcase to the hotel, she took Celine to the Tower, an elevator that extended one kilometer through the roof of the mall to a small dome above the city. The elevator flashed up to the dome so quickly that Celine felt nauseated. She kept her eyes closed until the elevator stopped, and when she opened them she was surprised that they were stepping into a small, darkened room.

"Just wait," her mom said.

Then the cement dome began to slide back, exposing a thick glass dome. It appeared to magnify the stars. She felt like they were almost close enough to touch.

"Turn around," her mom said, "and see your new world."

Celine did, and what she saw took her breath away! Before her was a huge, grayish blue ball floating in the dark. A thin line of darker blue appeared to circle it. Earth was twice the size of Mars! Huge patches of white shimmered in the sun. Her mom told her that they were lakes, and they were also blue but appeared shiny from space.

"It's so beautiful," she said. "And Mom, I am so glad I'll get to live with you."

Her mom wrapped her arms around her, giving her a big squeeze. Wrapped in her mom's arms, looking out at Earth, Celine felt safe and happy.

"Mom, you were right. Earth is astonishing."

"Yes, it is. And there are lots of wonderful experiences waiting there for you."

ABOUT THE AUTHOR

Jackie Hunter grew up in Richmond, Virginia, and worked as a school administrator and a middle school math/ science teacher in the Richmond area.

She is a lifetime member of The National Parent-Teacher Association. Ms. Hunter holds a Master of Education degree from Virginia Commonwealth University.

She is the author of *Lost in the Red Hills of Mars* where her literary techniques were compared to Ray Bradbury.

> *"A well-paced, diverting Mars survival adventure…*
> *blend of science and mystical fantasy."*
> – Kirkus Review

She lives in Las Vegas, Nevada.

For updates on releases and other information, you can find Jackie Hunter on her website: **JackieRHunter.com**

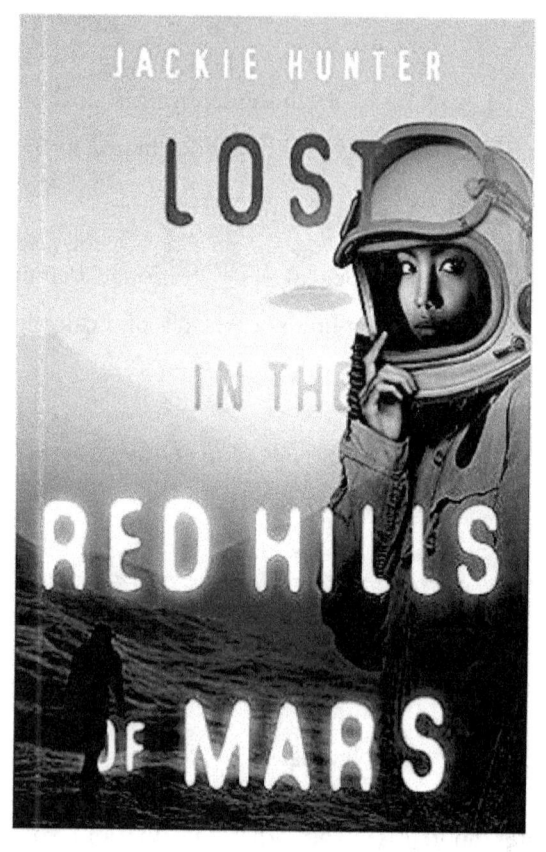

"A well-paced, diverting Mars survival adventure…
blend of science and mystical fantasy."
– Kirkus Review

www.ingramcontent.com/pod-product-compliance
Lightning Source LLC
Chambersburg PA
CBHW070808180626
46818CB00001B/155